SINGING BACK THE DARK

Singing Back the Dark

by

Simon Bestwick

Black Shuck Books
www.BlackShuckBooks.co.uk

First published in the UK by Black Shuck Books, 2018

978-1-913038-13-7

The Psalm

Grant kept walking as the air grew damp and cold. There didn't seem much point turning back, with Sheila gone. The house was bigger, colder, in her absence; the spaces she'd left in the drawers and wardrobe, where dresses, underwear, tights and shoes had been, gaped like wounds. It would've been easy to close them, sweep the stacks of socks, boxer shorts, hanger'd shirts and trousers, to fill the gaps. But he didn't. It'd be a final concession that her departure was permanent, one he knew he couldn't sustain if he made it now.

The moor stretched ahead, behind, on either side; from his left came the distant swishing of cars, back and forth along the motorway. He veered right, under the humming wires of a pylon; he wanted civilisation left far behind.

The damp air burned his lungs like petrol fumes. His cagoule flapped around him; his boots, sturdy and sensible, squelched in the mud. Moist wind stung his face.

It should just have been another Sunday. They'd go hiking, like they always did. Except he'd gone to B&Q yesterday and come home to find Sheila gone. He'd been buying shelving, to put up at her suggestion (it was gathering dust or damp in the garage now). That hurt most of all; she'd planned it, been waiting, suggested the shelving just to get him out of the house. When had she packed?

Not that it mattered. *Sheila, you bitch. Sheila, my love.*

He'd driven out across Lancashire, to the moors, and avoided the paths they normally took. Sheila had never been adventurous. He'd never thought of himself as such, either; curious, perhaps. That was what was drawing him out across the moor.

But it was November, and gone three o'clock; soon it'd be dark. Grant knew he should turn back while the path was easy to find; that it was easy to get lost. But he pressed on.

When he'd walked the anger, the bitterness

and the grief out of his system – at least for now – and focussed again on the world around him, he realised the air was the dull leaden grey of dusk. He looked at his watch; twenty to four. *Turn back.*

Which way? He turned. Double back, he presumed, but there were no landmarks. He couldn't even hear the traffic. A pylon, then – the powerlines would cross the motorway or human habitation at some point. He didn't want to die, lost and alone, of hypothermia. They'd say it was suicide, but he wouldn't give in so easily.

He looked around. But he couldn't see the pylon anywhere. There must be one, though; that faint humming sound he could hear, what else could it be?

Grant turned and started walking. His breath billowed whitely out ahead of him. But it wasn't the only white; to his dismay, he saw long white fingers of mist extending down either side of him. Looking back, he made out the white mass of it cresting the rise a hundred yards to his rear, seeping down.

Don't panic. Do not panic. If you panic, out here in this, you will die.

He started walking faster, back the way he'd

come. But *was* it the way he'd come? The ground was slippery and uneven. Could he have negotiated this without being aware of it, on autopilot? It didn't seem possible.

Uncertainty made him falter; he stopped, turned around, trying to get his bearings in the shrinking landscape. He listened through the blanketing mist, trying to hear something – the pylon's hum, distant traffic, anything...

He took a half-step back, and the ground slid under him. With a yelp he pitched backwards, arms flailing, body curling inward so as not to hit his head. He landed on his side; the earth knocked breath from his body and a protrusion of rock clipped his hipbone. His cry was only faint because he was winded; the pain was shocking and excruciating, almost numbing in its intensity.

Grant slid and rolled, arms and legs scrabbling for balance, trying to slow the descent. He'd no idea where the slope ended up, couldn't see from this angle; for all he knew it dropped straight into some deep gully carpeted in bare stone.

Luckily, it didn't. He landed in mud and soggy grass at the bottom of the slope, but slid further, into a sort of ditch. He half-slipped, half-rolled his way down, and came at last to rest on flat ground. He managed to stand, chest burning, hip throbbing.

Which way? Which way?

He couldn't tell; the mist was everywhere, wrapping him tight, mummifying him in damp air. *Oh fuck. Oh fuck.*

Mist distorts sound as well. The faint humming of the pylon – his one lifeline to the world – seemed to come from all around.

Must not panic.

Grant tried to gauge which way the ground sloped. If he could reach higher ground, he'd have a chance of seeing something. The motorway, or even a farmhouse. Surely he could beg shelter and warmth there?

One thing was certain: he couldn't stay put. He guessed at the direction of the incline and started walking; sure enough, the ground steepened, and as if in encouragement, the humming grew louder, although with no sign of the pylon through the mist.

Only, *was* it a pylon? He couldn't be sure now. Pylons hummed all right, but you usually had to be quite close to hear them, certainly within sight. He looked up; beyond the mist, the sky was a dirty, dishwater grey, sullen and gravid, uncrossed by wires.

So what *could* he hear? It was louder now, a little clearer even through the mists. It grew clearer still as he gained height, and as it did – was it just his imagination that the mists were thinning? – he made out its shape. The sound rose and fell – for a few seconds it was thinner, quieter, then for the same measure of time it swelled, louder. It was the only way to describe it. It sounded strangely familiar, but from where?

The mists were definitely thinning. Through the whiteout, the brow of a hill disclosed itself. The path was much steeper now, but Grant forced himself onwards, towards the clear spot.

The hum rose and fell, rose and fell. Something skittered and rustled below him, but when he looked back the mists were inscrutable. Probably just an animal of some kind; even so, he turned and walked faster.

At times it seemed that the path, ever steeper, would never reach the top, but he kept going. All he had to measure his progress by was the hum; it got louder and clearer as he went, and in doing so it heartened him, pushing him further on.

At last he reached the top. The landscape was pale and spectral; hills were hulking shadows in white veils of mist, the sky blackening, the light stealing quickly away now. But through the mist some of the closer hills seemed to be getting clearer. He prayed to the God of his childhood – long forgotten and discarded – that the mist might be receding.

His lungs burned, his legs shook. Sweat trickled down his back: *God, I am unfit*. Or just old, perhaps – getting there, anyway. His hip throbbed dully with what would surely be a spectacular bruise, soon enough.

The mist was like a – retreating? – sea, lapping around the peak he was on. He looked out across it, trying to hear the traffic, make out a pylon even, but he couldn't. *Christ, how far did I walk?* All he could hear was the humming sound. It was clearer than ever, now, from where he stood. The humming wasn't an unbroken note, he realised. It sounded like... words?

That was where he'd heard it. A television programme, on one of the Outer Hebrides. The religion was Calvinist, allowing no music except the human voice. A precentor sang the psalm's first line; the congregation sang it back. This sounded the same. The melody seemed flat, atonal, but perhaps that was the range and mist. A lone voice, then a chorus echoing it. A long way from the Hebrides, but still. A congregation – people. He could find them, shelter there.

He looked around again, and on the slopes below, he saw a shape in the mist. Thin, thinner than he'd seen anyone look outside footage of concentration camps, but human nonetheless.

Grant shouted, arms waving; the figure stopped, eerily still, then slowly turned. Although he couldn't see its face, he knew it was staring up at him.

As a long, cold moment gathered and broke, Grant realised calling its attention to him had been a mistake.

And as it began striding purposefully up the hill towards him, other shapes like it stole out of the mists.

Grant turned. He could run back down the other side of the hill, but he was facing an impenetrable wall of white vapour, and something dark was moving in it. Something long and thin, reaching out.

Grant recoiled from it, almost fell back down towards the other figures. Far from retreating as he'd hoped, the mist was rising, but he was almost glad of that; it kept the half dozen scarecrows making their slow but unrelenting ascent mercifully indistinct. With their long, spindly limbs they resembled spiders; as did the shape he'd recoiled from, which was moving out of the mist, advancing towards him along the hill's brow.

He turned and ran. The mist was still rising – at any moment something could step out of it, in front of him. Grant clenched his fists and ignored the pain in his hip – oh, for a good stout walking stick to lash out with, but he'd refused one out of pride. *Which goeth before a fall.*

On the slopes to either side there were shapes in the mist. He refused to look behind him, at what might be coming. He didn't want to see how close it was, or worse, what it looked like. He didn't know where his conviction came from that there would be far less flesh on its bones than there ever ought to be on a thing that moved , but while he badly wanted to be proved wrong, he didn't want to risk the alternative.

The brow of the hill was thinning, running

along a razor blade. Shocks of vegetation erupted in sprouts on either side, getting thicker and thicker. And higher. Thorn bushes – blackthorn, was it? Through the hoarse rasping of his breath, and the thumping of his heart, he heard the psalm grow louder.

It drove into him from the side; he whirled to face it. To his right, a narrow winding path was flanked by high thorn bushes that rose so high on each side they threatened to meet in a long-extended arch or cloister. The mist was a thin veil in the falling dark; the sound welled in it like blood in a wound. Down there, somewhere, Grant saw a gleam of light.

There was a rustling sound back along the ridge. Grant ran down the path, stumbling a couple of times, his own momentum carrying him on. He almost overbalanced, and had to catch at the bushes – pain ripped through his hand and he yelped again. The psalm didn't falter, though; it drew him on.

Grant stumbled onwards. The light gleamed through mist at the foot of the path, where the tunnel of blackthorn opened out. It didn't matter; between the light and the psalm, he had his beacon now.

Past the bushes there were trees; three or four yews, branches already bare, rose like outspread, skeletal hands. Pines rose up behind a small stone chapel; from a post outside it, an old-fashioned oil lamp swung. It was a small building, looked almost as if built from drystone, with a low triangular roof and a small steeple or bell-tower, little more than a shapeless lump at one end. The psalm drifted from its doorway.

The door itself was warped and almost spongy to the touch, blotched with moss and even a small cluster of fungus. Rust flaked from the iron ring serving it for a handle. Grant pushed it wide, and the psalm ceased.

The doorway opened out into a small, mean space. In the thick dusk, lit only by glimmers stealing in through the glassless windows, Grant saw pews each side of the aisle, little more than benches. At the far end was a raised dais with a bare table for an altar; no cross silhouetted against the broken window, threadbare carpet underfoot.

The silence hurt; like the mist thickening outside the windows, cloaking the dimming light, it had physical presence and force.

The psalm had led him here – how or why, he didn't know. But here was shelter, here was the chance of rest and getting warm, if...

Outside the light died, the lantern extinguished, and there were rustling and scraping sounds, like twigs or something almost as naked dragging over stones. Grant turned towards the door, and then he heard the psalm again.

It came from the altar, this time so loud it pushed against his back like hands, and he physically stumbled. When he turned, seven figures were standing on the dais, before the altar-bench.

At first he thought they must be nothing more than shadows and mist; he could see the altar-bench through them, the last dying light in the sky beyond. But then they were solid and there was no disputing them. They wore robes frayed and tattered at the sleeves and hems, worn and patched with mildew, and cowls that were deep cups of shadow, drowning their faces, for which Grant was thankful.

The tallest figure, in the centre, sang, although Grant couldn't make out the words or even the language. Its voice was the wind moaning in the hollow stone throat of a cave. The second it finished, the others echoed its song with their own.

The sleeves of their robes all met and overlapped and hid their hands from view, but that mercy was short-lived as the central figure – *the precentor*, Grant thought – stepped from the dais into the aisle, and the others followed. The figure to the left of it extended a pyx, the box that held the Host at Mass when Grant was a child, and the long scraping twigs of its free hand caught the lid and pulled it back to show Grant emptiness. The one to the right proffered a dulled pewter chalice.

The precentor reached under its robes. *The blood and the body*, Grant thought as it drew something out, something long, gleaming and sharp; *the blood and the body*.

In a moment he might see what was inside their cowls; that, as much as anything else, made him turn back towards the door. But it was already swinging open. The precentor sang another line, and the response this time was loudest of all, as the congregation filed in.

Ace Granchelet was leaning back against the tree-trunk, eyelids growing heavy, when the twig snapped underfoot and he was awake. The .38 stashed in his sock was in his hand almost before he knew it and aimed into the dark beyond the campfire's faint circle of light.

"Who's out there?" he called. "Come on out and show yourself now."

He regretted the words as soon as they left his mouth. There was no knowing who was out there. Could be white folks. White folks didn't take much to black folks pointing guns their way.

But some things you can't take back. Words are hard enough, but actions – well, you take out a gun and point it at a body, ain't something they're likely to forget.

Nothing left to lose, then. If whoever was out

there meant him harm, they'd come do it, or try to. Might as well be ready.

He clicked back the .38's hammer. It was a Saturday night special, nothing like the .45 he'd used in France back in '17. Once a soldier, always a soldier. You needed good equipment, Ace knew that, but this was all he could afford. For all he knew it'd blow up in his face when he pulled the trigger. He had a knife, too, tucked away up his sleeve – these days, a man didn't protect himself he was apt to end up dead. But a knife wasn't worth shit 'cept up close, 'less you threw it, and what if you missed, or if there was more than one?

"Come show yourself," he called again.

More twigs snapped and undergrowth rustled, and Ace damn near pulled the trigger there and then. *Easy boy. Don't shoot yet. Too keyed up. Too on-edge.*

Ace would've given his back teeth right then for a half-pint of sour mash or even a cigarette. But neither was to be had right now. Wouldn't be till he reached a town where they had work.

Branches rustling. His finger on the trigger. *Easy. Take it easy.*

The woman stepped out into the circle, barefooted and wearing a faded print dress. Her hands were out from her body, bare palms turned towards him. She had crinkly long dark hair and light brown skin – what they called high yellow. She looked sullen, tired, hungry and angry, and her face was dirty, but she could be pretty, he thought, if she gave it enough of a try.

"I ain't gonna hurt you," she said.

"I know *that*," Ace told her. "What you doing hiding out in the dark there?"

She shrugged. He put her in her early twenties, give or take; five, maybe ten years younger than him. "You bring any friends?" he asked. "Tell the truth now."

"I ain't got no friends, mister," she said. "It's just me."

Ace relaxed a little. "So what you doin' here?"

A knot cracked in the fire. Neither moved. Ace lowered the .38's hammer, and lowered the gun too, but kept it resting on his knee, just in case.

"I'm hungry," she said simply. Her eyes flicked towards the fire, and the spitted rabbit Ace'd caught. It was smelling good, and the smell would be drifting through the woods.

Ace pursed his lips, considering. Then he nodded and beckoned to her. "Come sit down, girl. Warm yourself awhile."

She shuffled forward, feet dragging in the mould. "How 'bout some of that rabbit?"

"We'll see."

She sat, crossing her legs awkwardly, the old dress riding up. She didn't have any panties on, and Ace looked away. *You don't go looking up a lady's dress*, his father said in the back of his head. *A man don't do such things.*

A small smile buckled the girl's lips, but she just said "Name's Ella."

"Uh-huh."

"Ella Warrens."

"Uh-huh."

"You got a name?"

"Uh-huh."

Ella snorted through her teeth, glanced away, shook her head. Ace smiled to himself. "Folks call me Ace."

She shrugged. "One name's good as another."

"Uh-huh."

"You ever say anything but 'uh-huh'?"

"Uh-huh," he said, and grinned. After a moment, she shook her head again, but this time she smiled too. Nice smile. Couple teeth missing, but no-one was perfect.

"You ain't from round here, are ya?"

"Nope. You?"

She nodded. "Couple miles from here. With my momma. Leastways, I did."

"Happened?"

"Shack burned down. Momma got kilt."

"Sorry to hear that."

Ella shrugged. "It's tough all over."

"Ain't that the truth."

"So whereabouts you from?"

"New Orleans. But I been all over."

"Where you come from?"

"Chicago. Hopped a freight train. Heard there was work going up in Detroit."

Ella laughed.

"What?"

"Hate to tell you, but you in Georgia."

"I know *that*." Ace scowled. "Hopped the wrong damn train."

Ella threw her head back and laughed some more. Had a pretty laugh too; chased the sullenness clean out of her face. She rocked back and her skirt hitched up, and for all Moses Granchelet'd taught his eldest boy, Ace couldn't resist stealing a glance this time.

"Why'd you get off here, anyways?" she finally asked. "Ain't *nothing* round these parts."

"Didn't have no choice. Railroad bull spotted me. Bastard started shooting at me – 'scuse my French – and weren't nothing to do but jump."

"Why didn't you shoot him?"

Ace snorted. "They ain't gonna miss a hobo falling off a train, but a railroad cop? I ain't dumb."

"You so smart, what you doing hopping the wrong train?"

"You want some of this rabbit or not?"

"Sorry, mister."

Ace grinned. It *had* been a pretty dumb mistake, at that. "Forget it."

"So... can I?"

"What?"

"Have some of that rabbit?"

Ace glanced at the carcass, turned it a little. "Ain't ready yet."

"How 'bout when it is?"

"We'll see."

"Uh-huh."

"Depends."

"On what?"

"Got any whisky?"

"Nope."

"Tobacco?"

"Mister, all I got is what you see."

The fire crackled in the silence. Ace's lips were dry and he licked them. "That right?"

Ella pushed the straps of the dress down over her shoulders. Her breasts were small and firm, small dark nipples tilted up. She looked across at him, chin held up high.

Ace licked his lips again. He heard his father's voice in the back of his head, but a man was still a man, whatever colour skin he had and whatever kind of God he had or hadn't got. "OK," he said.

Ella smiled and crawled around the campfire towards him.

2

Once they'd eaten Ace pulled his old Army blanket over them both. The fire was burning down. He mulled over whether he should get a little more wood for it.

It could wait either way. Right now he lay on his back with a full belly and a pretty girl curled up against his side. Ella's head lay on his shoulder, while his rested on his guitar case. He could've used a cigarette right about now, he reflected, but other than that things were about as good as they got for him lately.

The sky up above was clear, a million stars gleaming in the blue-black dark. Ella's hair tangled in his fingers as he ran them through it.

"Shit! Watch what you doing."

"Sorry, honey."

"Hm." Ella snuggled closer, tilted her head. "You play guitar?"

"Sometimes."

"Sing too?"

"Uh-huh."

"Uh-huh." She grinned. He smiled back and winked.

"Pays the rent now and again," he said. "Not all the time, though."

"Some of the time's better than none."

She yawned. "Maybe you could play for me, later?"

"What do I look like to you? You been fed. Din't say nothin' 'bout me takin' Molly out."

"Molly?"

"Uh-huh."

"You call your guitar Molly?"

"Uh-huh."

Ella laughed. Ace didn't, nor even smile. She stopped. "Why you call her that?"

He didn't answer.

"Well," Ella said at last, "maybe we could work something out." Her hand slid down over his flat belly.

"Ooh, yeah... maybe we could."

Her hand strayed back up to the curved ridge of a scar. "Happened there?"

"Got it in France. I was lucky. 'Nother inch I'd a been dead."

"You were in the War?"

"Uh-huh."

"What was it like?"

"Bad."

"You don't wanna talk about it, do ya?"

"Uh-huh."

"OK." Her hand slid back down. "Let's talk about you singing instead..."

A twig cracked, out in the dark. Ace went stiff, felt Ella go still in the crook of his arm. "You hear that?" she whispered.

"Uh-huh." It was little more than a breath. He moved his arm out from behind her head.

Crack.

Ace moved fast. He reached across to pick up

the .38, free hand buttoning his fly. "Get your dress back on," he whispered.

Another *crack* sounded. The first two had come from opposite sides of the clearing. This one had been right behind them. Ace's thumb found the .38's hammer again. He went still, listening.

"Ace?" Ella's voice was a whisper.

He held up a hand. "Hush."

Another twig snapped. Ace pivoted, aiming, but he didn't shoot.

Three at least. Maybe more. Just outside the clearing. Watching. This ain't good.

The hairs on the back of Ace's neck were up, despite the warm night. He'd been here before. France, and other places. The prickling hairs, the hollow clutching in the pit of his belly. Always before trouble started.

Five shots in the .38, if it didn't blow up in his face or misfire. And then there was the knife. He had to, he could fight with his hands or whatever they could take hold of. Kill with them too, it came to that.

If another twig cracked, he could fire, hit one of them maybe. But the rest? Chances were, there was 'least one gun pointing at Ace now.

Shoot and jump for it. Best chance you'll get.

A bead of sweat trickled down his temple.

To his right: *crack*.

Ace spun, aiming, pulling back the hammer, but then behind him came a crash of something tearing through the undergrowth, and Ella's scream. He spun to face it, saw a big body, a snarling bearded mouth, crazy eyes and a shotgun butt arcing towards his face. Then he was on his back and counting the millions of stars above him, till all of a sudden they all went out.

3

Something was stroking his back, up and up and up, the fingers never trickling back down again to start from scratch. Like two or three women, maybe. There'd been that whorehouse in France, that time. The girls liked trying out the black boys. Next day they were back at the front, and two of the boys he'd gone there with, Tela and Obie, both ended up dead; Tela with a German bayonet in the throat, Obie blown to pieces by a mortar shell.

Something dug into his back, hard, then clipped the back of his head.

Ace didn't make a noise, but he was awake. He couldn't breathe through his nose and there was blood in his throat.

The stars were above him again, but they were moving, running past like they were in flight. So were the tree branches.

Ace kept limp as it dawned. He was being dragged through the forest by the legs, arms trailing behind him.

He looked down the length of his body and saw two broad backs. The men were walking, each gripping an ankle. Between them he dimly made out two more men some way up ahead. They were dragging Ella the same way, only face down. Her skirt had rucked up to show her bare ass to the sky. Her hair and arms trailed in the dirt. She wasn't moving, but neither had he been a minute ago. One of the men was carrying something over his shoulder: Ace's first thought was that it was a gun, but the shape was wrong. Too bulky.

Then he realised: *Molly*.

Ah, shit.

The man holding his right leg had a shotgun propped on his shoulder. Looked like a

Winchester pump – he'd seen them in France. Trench brooms, they'd called them.

The one holding his left leg had a small-bore rifle. One of them most likely had the .38 as well. What about the knife? Only way to check was to reach over for his sleeve, but if the movement alerted them…

Only gonna get one chance.

Slow, ugly pain throbbed outward from his nose; the space between and behind his eyes felt packed with cotton wool.

Motherfucker broke my nose.

Forget that for now.

He lolled his head back and as far as he dared to the side.

The dirt track behind him was empty.

Good thing too, dumbass; there had been, they'd've seen you were awake.

First job was to get himself free and clear. He couldn't take all four of them, even with the knife. But he could follow them back to wherever they were going. Then… what?

Run get the cops, maybe. Or just run.

Shame on you, thinking that, his father told him. *'Specially after you took advantage of that poor girl.*

No, he wasn't going to leave Ella if he could help it. He'd no idea what these bastards had in mind, but it couldn't be anything good. By the time he could find a cop – assuming they had any interest in a black woman's fate – Ella could be dead.

That left it all up to him.

He could almost see his father nod approvingly. Not that his father would have raised his *voice* to a white man, let alone a hand. He'd have considered that to be the short way to an appointment with a tree and a length of rope if he was lucky, or a jug of kerosene poured over him and his privates cut off if he wasn't.

But a man did certain things. His father taught him that. A man took care of his own, and paid what he owed.

The traitor thought crossed his mind: *you don't owe her shit.* He'd fed her; she'd paid for it, only way she could. That made them all square and nothing owing.

But that was bullshit and he knew it.

That's right, Isaac. Now you do what you got to do.

The man with the Winchester – he'd be most dangerous. Good gun like that, you gave it to the man could use it best. Take him first.

Ace ran what had to happen next through his head, glanced left and right. Thick woods lay dark on either side of them. A stone clipped the back of his head; he bit his lip to stop crying out, kept his legs limp with an effort.

No more time for thinking, Ace. Get doing.

It was a big hand and beefy that held his right ankle, but a loose grip. A fast move would tear him free.

Do it.

Ace yanked his right leg in towards him, ankle snatching loose of the big man's grip. The man turned, trying to get the shotgun round, and Ace glimpsed the snarling face he'd seen before.

He drove his right leg back out again, aiming at the side of the knee joint. His heel slammed home. Something cracked; the big man screamed high and loud and fell back, shotgun firing upwards.

The two men up ahead turning, dropping Ella's legs, scrabbling for their guns. One was older, whip-thin, a white scar snaking across his face and through his beard, the other squat and bald with an undershot jaw.

The man holding Ace's left leg let go of it,

gawping. He looked no older than nineteen; a slack, foolish face, without nose, chin or forehead to speak of. But even a boy could kill if the gun was pointing the right way, and the rifle was swinging to bear.

Ace knocked the barrel aside with his left hand, punched the boy hard as he could in the balls with his right, then tumbled him sideways over the big man and rolled for the trees.

Shouts.

"See him?"

"Shoot! Shoot!" The bellowing voice was as full of agony as of rage – the big man. "Kill the fucking nigger!"

Ace was up and running. Moon and starlight picked the trees out, but if he could see them...

Gunshots behind him. He dived, scrabbling through the earth; bullets whipped overhead, buckshot spattered the tree boles. Then he upped and ran again, keeping low. His back tingled, waiting for the bullet. He grabbed a tree and ducked behind it, pressing flat to the bark.

"See him?"

"Fuck!"

Ace fumbled up his left sleeve and found the haft of the knife. Something between a snarl and a grin pulled his lips back from his teeth as he pulled it free. He tensed and crouched to run or fight.

"You see him, Cephas?"

"Cain't see shit."

"We goin' after him?"

"Sure thing, you dumb shit. Be my guest."

Silence.

"Get this bitch back home with us. Floyd, help your brother walk."

"You OK, Clinton?"

"What you fucking think, you dumb bastard? My fucking leg. Eat that bastard's fucking liver. Help me walk."

"What about him, Cephas?"

"Go after him in the mornin'. He'll be lost in these woods. Tell a city nigger when I see one. We'll come lookin', and we'll find him." Cephas's voice rose. "You hear me, nigger? We're gonna come looking for ya. And we're gonna find you. And when we do, you'll wish you hadn't run."

Pain throbbed through Ace's head, but he bit his lip and gripped hold of the knife, listening out. The shouting could all be a trick. Trying to sneak up on him.

"Come on. Let's go."

Footsteps receding, and the big man's curses with him.

Ace waited until the woods were silent again. Then he slid down and sat against the tree-trunk. He put the knife in his mouth and bit down hard. Put his hands to his face; felt the bridge of his nose. His fingers encountered a bump and a blinding white flash like the end of the world burst across his vision. He bit down harder, took a deep breath, and yanked down, choking back the scream. It seemed to take an eternity of agonies to set the broken bone back into place, but at last he did, slumped back against the trunk with tears and blood pouring down his face. He sat there, breathing deep, till the pain ebbed enough to let him think.

4

They were expecting him to run.

Or try to, at least. *A city nigger*, the one called Cephas had called him. Not someone who'd know the woods. Someone who'd get hopelessly lost, and end up crying pitifully, waiting for them to come and finish him off.

Only he hadn't been raised in the city. And even if he had, he'd been a soldier. They were underestimating him, and that was good. Best weapon an enemy could give you.

'Course, a gun wouldn't hurt either.

He should get after them sooner rather than later. Every minute wasted brought Ella closer to death. But they knew these woods; *that* was a powerful weapon too. They were underestimating him; if he did the same for them he'd be dead.

So Ace waited, trying not to think of Ella while he did.

First light came at last, and he moved out onto the dirt track. He wanted to follow it, but didn't, not yet. Instead he turned and went back the way they'd come.

~

Ace was a good tracker. The military taught a man to be observant; besides which, he'd been out hunting small game with his father almost since he was old enough to walk.

So it wasn't hard to find the disturbed earth, leaves and undergrowth where the trail left the path. He followed it all the way back to the clearing.

He'd been pretty sure what he'd find, but had to check. And he was right; he found only the fire's remains, the rabbit's bones, and the Army blanket he'd covered them both with.

He'd nursed the tiny hope of finding the .38. It would've flown out of his hand when the big one – Clinton – knocked him down. In the dark, they might've missed it...

But it was gone.

And so was Molly.

They'd left the blanket, though. Couldn't blame them for that – it was a sorry-looking piece of rag, old, stained and smelly. But he could've lived without the blanket.

Not Molly, though. And they'd taken her.

Ace breathed in and out through his nose. It hurt; that made him angrier.

Stop that now, soldier. Get your shit together and think.

He nodded to himself. He had the knife, the skills he'd learned, and the fact they'd expect him to be running like hell, or whimpering and lost in the woods; he had all that on his side.

'Sides, last thing they'd expect him to do was come back for his woman. They thought of him as little better than an animal; what did animals know about loyalty or love?

Not that Ella was his woman as such, nor could he say he loved her. But what they'd done together had been sweet. And her smile and laugh had been sweeter still.

Even if she was alive and he could save her, chances were he'd never see her again. He was just passing through; he had no home, no job. It was work enough keeping himself alive and clothed and fed, never mind a woman as well. But still...

Forget that shit, soldier. That's a whole 'nother hill to take; you got to get past this one first.

Ace nodded again. He patted the knife sheathed on his left forearm, then turned and walked away from the clearing, back to the dirt track.

They've had Ella three, maybe four hours now. Whatever they'd got planned wasn't gonna end with either of us living to tell of it. If she ain't dead yet, she will be soon.

But that, too, was another hill to take.

But he allowed himself one more thought on the subject before following their trail:

If she ain't living when I get there, none of them will be when I leave.

5

Ace tracked them along the dirt trail best part of a mile, switching attention every few steps from the ground to the path up ahead, ears straining for the slightest sound, in case they'd started their hunt for him. Once a twig cracked; he stepped off the path and crouched, slipping the knife from its sheath, but less than a minute later a rabbit hopped from the undergrowth. Ace breathed out.

Well, might've been your daddy I ate last night. If so, consider us even.

The trail stopped abruptly at a bend in the path where a six-foot slab rose from the ground, topped with a gnarled oak whose roots straggled free of the earth to hang down like a nest of snakes.

Ace studied the rock face. It was canted at a steep angle, but a body could climb it if they were so minded. And rock didn't take footprints.

Something caught his eye; he reached up, plucking it free of the root it'd snagged on. He held it to the light: a long, crinkly hair.

Ella.

Ace pressed flat against the rock face, ear

cocked upward, listening. He heard nothing but birdsong. He gripped a couple of the thicker roots and hauled himself up to peer over the top of the slab.

The ground sloped down. It was thickly wooded and there was no clear path, not at first. They'd taken care not to beat one. Probably never took the exact same route twice, they could help it.

But if you knew where to look, that helped. With no beaten path, you couldn't *not* leave a sign. A broken twig here, a scuffed footprint there. Another strand of Ella's hair snagged on a tree's bark. Blood smeared on a rock. Hers? Clinton's?

Not much, anyway. She was hurt bad, there'd've been more.

'Less she was dead already.

Ace's flicked his hand like he was swatting a fly, and the thought left him, same as a fly would.

Couldn't climb down too fast. This was their turf now, more than ever; for all he knew they were watching him. He thought of the boy's game rifle, imagined it aimed at his temple.

Brushed that thought aside too.

A distant sound of running water, getting louder as he went.

He picked his way slowly down through the trees, glancing around for watchers.

He was looking around when his foot met only empty air and pitched him forward.

"Shit!"

It only came out as a hiss through his teeth, but a bluejay skittered from the tree he grabbed onto to keep from falling. Ace pulled himself back behind the trunk.

The ground dropped away sharply, a sheer face of rock. The running water was directly beneath him too. Water ran down the rockface into a pool; a little rill wove down from it to an old farmhouse's overgrown ruins. The roof fallen in, windows and doorway empty, one wall half-collapsed. Fragments of stone brick strewed the ground, snarled in creepers and saplings.

The hairs on the back of Ace's neck prickled up; the old familiar knot tied itself slowly in his stomach.

He held his breath, waited and watched.

And Clinton limped out of the ruins, raising the shotgun.

Ace's first thought was, the big bastard was lucky to be walking. The second was that he'd been seen.

But he hadn't. Not yet. Clinton was merely looking up in his direction because that was where the bluejay had been scared from. He was huge; six-four if an inch and close on three hundred pounds, precious little of it appearing to be fat.

Looks like his Momma fucked a grizzly bear.

Clinton put the shotgun to his shoulder, inched the barrel left and right, then shook his head and lowered the gun.

"Everythin' OK, Clinton?"

The whip-thin, scar-faced man stepped out of the ruins. He held a shotgun too; double-barrelled, maybe 10-gauge.

"Jest thought I heard something."

"Thinking it's the nigger?" Cephas's stained beard split in a grin. "Hell, he's *far* away b'now. Else he's runnin' round the woods soilin' his britches."

"Shit I hope so."

Cephas giggled. "Got a real hard-on for his black ass, don'cha?"

Clinton wheeled. "You callin' me a faggot?"

"Don't be any dumber'n you kin help, bro." Cephas clapped Clinton on the shoulder. "We'll get him. Think you can walk, that leg?"

"Just watch me. Gonna kill me that nigger *slow*."

Sweat ran down the runnel of Ace's spine.

"Ma wants us both downstairs," Cephas said. "Got work to do."

"Be there direc'ly."

"Wants us *now*, Clinton."

"*Said*, I'll be down direc'ly."

Cephas shrugged. "Up to you. Don't be too long now."

The whip-thin man disappeared back inside.

Clinton walked a ways from the house, turned, looked about. He wandered over towards the rockface and the pool. Ace kept behind the tree.

After a while, the scent of cigarette smoke rose to him.

Ace peeked down. Clinton sat on a tree stump, over to Ace's left at the pool's edge, shotgun across his knees. He had his back to Ace, gazing towards the farmhouse.

Ace was stood at the rockface's highest point.

To his left it sloped downwards. The lowest point was almost directly behind Clinton.

A slow, cold smile crossed Ace Granchelet's lips. He put the knife between his teeth, stepped back from the tree and began creeping slowly down.

~

The descent was slow; he had to watch literally each footstep. Check the ground for twigs, then Clinton's back, then the ground again. A slow, careful step. Clinton again. Then the ground, for the next step.

He didn't think of Ella as he descended, or look at the shotgun across Clinton's knees. Thinking of Ella wouldn't help him do what he had to, and the shotgun wasn't the danger. It couldn't kill him if Clinton was dead.

Clinton flicked away his cigarette, slapped his knees. Ace went still. He was five paces from the big man. Not far, but with his knife against Clinton's shotgun it might have been a mile.

Clinton drummed thick fingers on meaty thighs. Then he took out a leather tobacco pouch, opened it and began rolling himself another smoke.

Ace smiled around the knife.

So close now. The temptation to move faster was overpowering, but he resisted. Every nerve sang as he looked from Clinton to the ground and back again. At any moment the big man would turn.

Three paces. Clinton took out a cigarette lighter. Ace studied it. It must have been valuable once. Not so much now, battered and scuffed as it was. Still, it struck first time. Clinton touched it to his cigarette.

Two paces.

Clinton puffed the cigarette into life. The tobacco's rich scent rose again.

Take the pouch and lighter too. I could use a smoke.

Ace banished the thought. Tempting fate to think even a moment ahead.

He glanced over at the farmhouse; at any moment Cephas might emerge to holler his brother indoors. No movement. Then a sound from Clinton.

Shit.

He looked down. Clinton was stuffing the pouch and lighter back inside his clothes.

Ace breathed out. Just a little.

One pace.

He looked from the ground to Clinton, took the final step. Directly behind the big man. The sky was grey. No shadows on the ground.

Ace crouched and took the knife from between his teeth.

At the last second Clinton seemed to sense something and start to move, but it was too late. Ace's left hand seized the thick greasy mop of hair; his right drove the blade hilt-deep into the base of Clinton's skull.

A strangled, gagging noise came out of Clinton's throat; his hands half-rose, fingers hooked, as his whole body locked rigid. Then his arms dropped and the massive body pitched forward. Ace let go of knife and hair to avoid being dragged after him.

Clinton's body thudded into the leaf mould. His legs shuddered and twitched, then were still. A loud *brrrap* resounded through the clearing as his bowels failed; a bird took flight. A thick stench rose and Ace damn nearly gagged.

The bird's wings clattered like rulers.

Ace jumped to crouch beside the tree stump. The shotgun lay under Clinton. He heaved at the huge dead weight, all the while looking back up at the farmhouse. No-one came out.

Clinton flopped onto his back. His eyes bulged wide in his face and his mouth yawned open.

Ace took the shotgun. The butt of a pistol protruded from Clinton's waistband; Ace pulled it free. A Colt .45 automatic. He'd used one in France, snatched from a dead officer to use in a trench fight. He checked the clip and action. The chamber was empty. He pumped a round into it, put the safety on and thrust it through his belt at the back.

He checked the shotgun next. The chamber was loaded.

He left the knife in Clinton.

Ella.

Time to move.

He stood and walked towards the farmhouse.

7

"Clinton?"

The high, thin voice rang out of the ruins.

Shit.

Ace ducked down and sprinted towards the building, flattening himself against the broken wall.

"Clinton? Ma wants ya."

Didn't sound like he'd been heard.

"Clinton, quit foolin'... around..."

The voice trailed off. A thin figure shuffled round the wall. The boy with the rifle, eyes fixed on the body.

"Clinton?"

The boy took three steps forward. His back was to Ace now. The narrow shoulders lifted for a shout. Ace stepped forward and drove the stock of the shotgun into the back of the boy's skull.

Bone crunched and the boy dropped without a sound, shuddering. Ace slammed the stock down twice more. When he was sure the boy was dead, he cleaned the butt on the grimy bib overalls.

Then he went into the farmhouse.

The building was an empty shell, but a trapdoor gaped in the centre of the overgrown floor.

Ace crouched beside it. Faint noises drifted up. And smells – a thick, choking reek of smoke. Beneath that was the stink of sweat and grease, shit, and rotten things, but also cooking odours – some kind of meat that, despite everything, made his stomach growl.

The hairs on the back of his neck prickled like never before.

A ladder led down to an earth floor. Thin yellow light flickered across it.

Ace took a deep breath. If he'd still believed in God he would've said a prayer. But he didn't.

So he shinned down the ladder without another thought.

He dropped to the earth floor, swinging the shotgun left and right.

The empty space might've been a root cellar once. Two tunnels led off from it. They looked to have been dug out by hand. Tree roots dangled from the ceiling. The greasy yellow light flickered round the tunnel's bends.

Which one?

Go left first.

He turned; his foot caught something.

He looked down.

It was a fingerbone.

If it'd just been that, the breath wouldn't have caught in his throat. But it lay beside a pit in the floor, and the pit was full of yellowed whitish things.

Some of them were split across the crown.

And they grinned.

Beside them there were two other pits, just the same.

Ace choked down the sickness in his throat.

It'd been at the back of his mind: *why?* What did they want with two no-account Negroes with no money and nothing else of value, 'less you counted Molly?

Now he knew.

Ella.

If she's dead, they all die. I'll leave nothing alive in this place.

He took the left-hand tunnel.

Alcoves had been hollowed out in the walls. They were stacked with things. Bundles of clothes, guns; there were shovels and pitchforks, knives, forks, plates.

At the end of the tunnel, in the newest, half-filled alcove, he found Molly.

He stroked the worn wood of the guitar case.

"I'll come back for you, honey," he whispered.

He walked back to the root cellar.

The right-hand tunnel faced him. Yellow light flickered balefully in its depths.

Left one's where they store their takings. The right... the right's where they live.

Where they cook.

His palms sweated. He wiped them on his worn suit, one hand, then the other. Then he started down the tunnel.

"Floyd? That you?"

A shadow flickered at the tunnel's bend.

"Clinton?"

Ace stood still, said nothing.

From round the bend came the click of hammers thumbed back.

"Who's that?"

Ace raised the shotgun.

And Cephas leapt out into the tunnel, crouching, the 10-gauge aimed out ahead of him.

When the shot came, it exploded in the tunnel like thunder.

8

Cephas hit the tunnel wall and shot the ceiling. Dirt rained down on him as he dropped to the floor. Blood bubbled from his lips and what remained of his chest, but he fumbled at his waistband and a long-barrel revolver slid into view.

Ace worked the slide on the Winchester, hardly hearing its *click-clack*, not hearing the tinkle of the empty shellcase falling at all over the singing in his ears, and fired again.

Cephas's face disappeared and blood sprayed up the ceiling. The revolver dropped from his fingers. His body dropped sideways and was still.

There was screaming, over the singing in his ears – *to your right, Ace.*

He whirled, pumping the slide, and aimed the shotgun into a chamber just ahead and to his right.

A scrawny black-haired woman scrambled back from him, screaming, spitting and clutching a skinny, wild-haired child – maybe eleven or twelve, and Ace couldn't see if it was a boy or a girl.

Movement at the far end of the tunnel – Ace wheeled away from them. The squat, bald man looked up from Cephas, eyes wild, and screamed. A pistol swung up in his hand.

Ace fired. The squat man shrieked and hurled himself back round the bend in the tunnel. Ace walked forward, jacking the slide, shouting things he could barely hear himself, much less make sense of.

The hair on the back of his neck – he turned and an axe arced towards his face.

Ace threw himself sideways against the tunnel wall, the axe slashing by, the scrawny woman swerving to face him and raising it again. Her face, slack and chinless, rotted teeth bared in a scream – he fired and blew her back down the tunnel, in through the entrance of the chamber she'd come out of.

Wild eyes in the smoke, a scream over gunfire's echo in his ears, a knife lunging towards his belly. Ace pumped the slide and fired again, seeing the child's face in the second before it vanished, blown apart into red pulp, the small body blown backwards across its mother's.

Oh Jesus Christ mother of fucking God I just killed a fucking kid—

A blow whacked into his upper left arm, spun and slammed him against the wall, the shotgun spinning from his hands.

Blood pouring down his fingers. At the end of the tunnel the squat man screamed and fired again.

Ace bellowing, a bullet brushing his ear, an inch from killing him, as he scrambled over the dead mother and child into the antechamber.

Footsteps thudding on the earth floor – he pulled the .45 from his belt, put it in his left hand, steadied it with his right, pointed it round the corner and fired two, three times. The recoil was brutal, driving the gun up each time, pain screaming from his wrist, but the squat man screamed too.

Silence.

Moaning and whimpering. A slithering sound.

Ace looked out. The squat man's legs vanished round the bend of the tunnel. The pistol lay fallen amid splashes of blood.

Ace took the .45 in his right hand and walked. Pain throbbed in his left arm; the fingers of the hand were blood-slick, but he felt calm, easy. Blood hammered in his ears.

He rounded the corner, pointed the gun ahead.

The squat man was writhing back down the tunnel, away from him. He'd been hit in the stomach and was bleeding out over the tunnel floor. When his mouth opened to shriek, it was full of blood, like a nightmare wound full of teeth.

Ace aimed the .45 down at that mouth.

The squat man screamed and threw up a pleading hand.

Ace fired through the hand. Three fingers blew off it and blood vomited from the ugly mouth and out through the back of the head. The squat man's body slammed flat to the floor and was still.

Silence. Just the keening whine in his ears.

No. Not quite.

There was another keening noise. A voice.

Ace walked slowly. The tunnel came to a dead end a dozen yards beyond the squat man's corpse, but a yard or two beyond the body was a final antechamber. The keening noise wailed out of there, a one-note sound of terror, agony and madness.

"Ella?" Ace called.

Just as the wailing rose over the whine in his ears, so something overrode the stench of blood and shit and cordite in his nostrils. Smoke. And the smell of cooking.

Ace staggered into the last chamber and swayed.

A fire roared in a huge, crude, unventilated fireplace at the back. Smoke hazed the air.

Something squatted in a corner of the room.

Naked, grub-pallid, vastly obese. Thin, stringy grey hair clung to its scalp; pendulous breasts hung to its navel. Thin, stick-like arms pawed at the air. A mouthful of blackened teeth yawned in a scream. The eyes were tiny black dots, without whites or irises, like a maggot's. If it had legs, they were lost beneath its bloated gut, only a tiny, claw-like pair of feet protruding.

Beside it, a huge steel pot hung above another fire. It bubbled and steamed foully.

Ma's waiting.

"Ella!" Ace's voice frightened him. It was a scream, close to the madness of the one wailing out of the thing in front of him. "Ella! What did you do with her, you—"

The smell of cooking.

The fireplace – something about the fireplace.

Ace stared around the room, saw old, scattered bones. But he saw other things. A hook in the ceiling. A chain looped through it. Tin pails, brimming with something dark and wet...

The fireplace...

A spit above the fire, and there was something skewered on it. A carcass on it, big...

Something bobbing in the pot, something covered with something long and straggly...

The fireplace...

The fire, the carcass – so what, already seen it...

No...

The fireplace...

No, not the fireplace...

Something beside the fireplace.

A stained, bundled piece of cloth...

The pattern on the cloth.

A faded pattern he'd seen before.

Wheeling back to the mother – to the *thing* – and she – *it* – was screaming.

And Ace Granchelet was screaming too.

Screaming as he aimed the .45...

Screaming as he fired...

Still screaming long after the gun was clicking empty...

Still pulling the trigger.

9

Outside the farmhouse the air was clean and sweet.

Birds sang.

The little rill bubbled past the ruins.

Ace moved slowly.

He was almost done.

He'd cleaned and bandaged the wound in his left arm. A little stiff, but he figured he'd be OK.

Molly lay on the ground. With her was the .45.

Clinton's tobacco pouch and papers too.

He took nothing else from that place.

He could barely bring himself to take the gun and tobacco, but it didn't pay for a man to go unarmed, and Ace figured the least he deserved was a smoke.

He figured Ella wouldn't have grudged him that.

But nothing else.

He'd dumped Clinton and Floyd into the root cellar and dragged the trap shut. It was well-hidden among the weeds of the farmhouse floor. He could almost believe it'd never been real. None of it.

Almost.

He'd brought one other thing up from below, but with no intention of keeping it. A shovel.

He'd thrown it into the pool when he was done.

He rinsed his hands over and over in the

stream, till they were chapped and sore. Despite the washing, it felt as through the grease still clung to his hands. From the thing from the fireplace. The thing from the pot.

The dirt was pounded flat atop the hole he'd dug. The cross he'd lashed together was crude, but it'd stand awhile at least. The flat piece of wood fixed to it held a name and a date: today's, the 3rd of August 1931. More than that he didn't know. Didn't even know her right age.

He'd vomited two or three times in the process, but it'd been a thing he'd had to do. He couldn't have left her down there, with them.

And it was a penance of a kind. For being too late.

Ace dragged his sleeve across his eyes.

He was done here.

He rolled a cigarette, lit and smoked it. Put the tobacco in his pocket and the .45 in his belt. Then he picked up Molly and started walking.

10

Ace walked a ways; he wasn't rightly sure afterward how far or long, but came a time he found a railroad and followed till he could see a station. He sat in the grass and waited.

Soon enough, a train came.

He climbed aboard a freight car as the train slowed down and prayed he wouldn't find another railroad bull like the last one; he wasn't rightly sure he'd restrain himself from shooting this time.

If there was a bull, Ace's guess was he was taking it easy, because he passed the journey unmolested.

He rolled a couple of cigarettes and smoked them, running a hand over Molly's case.

Then he opened it, took out the smooth, red, polished guitar and laid it across his knees.

He took a deep breath, then held the neck of the guitar in his left hand, flexing the fingers, testing them for stiffness. His right hand toyed with the strings.

Then, as the freight train rattled across America toward its unknown destination, Ace Granchelet, slow tears rolling down his cheeks, picked out a mournful tune on the guitar he called Handsome Molly, and sang a slow, sad song for a high-yellow gal by the name of Ella Warrens.

All the window showed him was his own reflected face. That and the room behind – two cards on the mantelpiece and the small, barely-decorated tree with its scrubby, threadbare tinsel and half-dozen plastic baubles covered in cheap gilt already almost scratched away, the sole visible concessions to the season.

Tucked away behind a pub, the Close was a small still pocket in the busy city's heart. Only five houses, and all but his was empty tonight. No lights left on to ward off thieves, even: foolish. Chris could have sworn that Harry and Ella at number three had set up some sort of timer to activate the houselights at intervals, but if so, it wasn't working.

Chris sipped his coffee; it was cold. He considered enlivening it with a dash of Bell's, but resisted; the picture would have been too miserable, alone in the silent, cluttered house. No matter. There was the CD player, the DVD: devices to fill the house with sound and light.

He was standing over the CD player, trying to choose between Purcell and Monteverdi, when his phone rang. Loud in the silence, it made him jump. He fumbled the phone up, squinted at its screen, then answered the call. "Julia," he said.

"Chris." Her voice was blurred by washes of static; it sounded like waves breaking on shingle. "I just wanted to see how you were."

"I'm okay."

"And to say... you know, the offer still stands. You can still come over, I mean," she said. "The service isn't for another hour. We'd love to see you."

We: he didn't even know who *we* were. Her mother, father, sister, child – or did she have a boyfriend, girlfriend, husband, wife? He'd never been sure, never known how to ask without seeming gauche and clueless. The number of times he'd blundered into humiliation, embarrassment – he could hear the mocking playground laughter in his ears, even at thirty years' remove. The potential friendships he'd ruined by misreading the signs, the opportunities missed through blindness, timidity and second-guessing.

The carol service tempted him nonetheless. Once he'd have snorted at it as foolishness or superstition, but now it called to him. It brought back memories of Christmas as something other than a festival of consumerism and gluttony. That thought sounded dour and staid, even to him, the voice of some cold grey man who wanted to banish all the season's cheer, but he knew there was truth in it as well, that the Christmas he knew now was as joyless as any zealot's marking of the season. It had once been different; a time of happiness and light. There'd been a beauty and a mystery to it when he'd been a boy, when his parents had been alive – far beyond anything he could understand. He'd sung in the school choir and warm candlelight had filled the space, gleaming off the brass cross on the altar and the high stained-glass windows. There'd been a togetherness, something warm against the night outside that he couldn't define, and missed. Would it be at the church tonight, if he went, or would it be absent even there and make the season bleaker still?

"That's very kind of you," he said – stilted, formal. Both of them, picking tentatively over the landscape as if through a minefield. He was almost certain that Julia might be interested in him in that way, in the way he thought of her. Almost, but not quite, and in that word there was a great gulf fixed. And when you'd been burned so many times, venturing out got harder. Your own four walls, void and cheerless as they were, were at least comforting and familiar. Better than someone else's home, full of traps waiting to be sprung. "But I'm fine."

"It's no trouble," Julia said. "Really."

A part of him wanted to; the rest was too afraid to hope and besides, her home, only a short walk away, abruptly seemed a vast and insuperable distance, reached only by an effort beyond his meagre physical resources. That nebulous hope was outweighed by the dread of disappointment and humiliation, and the comforts of home, devised to compensate for that lack, were suddenly irresistible in their allure. "I think I'll stay in," he said at last. "I'll let you know in the morning about dinner. If that's all right."

"It's fine," she said. Was she angry or sad, her voice dull with annoyance or muted with regret?

"I'll talk to you tomorrow, then. Merry Christmas."

"Merry Christmas."

The phrase meant something to him, even now, with any faith he'd had long left behind. Back then the shepherds and the wise men, the angels and the child, Mary and Joseph – all this had been real and true, history, as integral to life as breath and bread, water or wine. No division or separation: all one thing.

Now? Only appetite, nothing else; an excuse for it, all else a gloss on the turd, a means to an (arse) end. The worst of it, of course, was the fear that it had never been what he remembered, had always been like this. Chris folded the phone and pocketed it, then turned back to the stereo. Neither Monteverdi nor Purcell, he decided, tonight; the Baroque composers could await another day. There was a CD of Christmas carols. If he couldn't be at the church with Julia, he could at least bring the music to him and see if it stirred whatever it was that lay dormant in him. He put it on, let the music break the house's silence.

Perhaps he was being foolish, or cowardly. Timid again, afraid to venture anything. He reached into his pocket, touched the phone. Perhaps he should call Julia back, tell her he'd changed his mind.

He flicked the phone open, and the lights went out; on the stereo, *I Saw Three Ships* was cut off in mid-verse.

Banging his shins on the furniture, Chris blundered in search of the fusebox, but then looked out of the window – he and the room were now faint ghosts in the glass – to see the darkness outside was now absolute. A couple of streetlamps, visible from the house, had also gone out, and the sky, where the clouds had burned a dull orange with reflected sodium light, was black now too.

Not the fusebox, then: a power cut. He couldn't remember the last time such a thing had happened – it might have been far back in his childhood. Candles and board games; reading by candlelight. An adventure, it'd felt like. Flipping open the phone, he used its thin pale glow to navigate to the kitchen, where he found candles and kitchen matches in the drawers.

Once lit, and anchored to plates and saucers by congealing puddles of dripped wax, the candles filled the living room with a dim warm glow – far dimmer than the extinguished lights, but warmer. Old memories, fond ones. Chris sat in the candlelight, splashed Bell's into a mug, reached for a paperback.

The faint candlelight pushed a little of the dark back from the window, but it flickered, so that there always seemed to be movement, just out of Chris' sight. He kept looking up at first, before forcing himself to concentrate on his book.

He didn't know what made him look up again; maybe he sensed on some level that the latest flicker he'd seen was something more than a dancing flame. He looked up, through the window, and saw the shadows outside starting to move.

People, filing into the Close. Carol singers? But such people always missed the Close – it was too well-hidden – and besides, they were silent. At first he thought they had no lights with them, either, but dull orange motes like coals or embers seemed to swim in the air about them.

Christmas had always been the one night when, as a boy, he was free of ghosts – no monsters under the bed, in shadowed corners or the night outside, only Santa Claus and Rudolph, the Christ Child and the three wise men, following their star across the desert. Ghost stories for Christmas had been pleasures, not nightmares, because that night they weren't real. Even with his childhood faith long fallen away, it felt to Chris like a violation for this time of the year to hold any kind of menace.

Chris stood, went closer to the window. The skins of those shapes in the dark looked grey, their tattered garments black. The lights, though; what were those lights?

And then one of them rose right in front of him and pressed its face to the window, and Chris saw the lights came from its eyes and mouth, or the ragged holes that served for them. Its hairless, noseless head was like a great clump of cigarette ash, lit from within by a still-glowing ember. Its long hands spread across the glass. The candles flickered, and something else spread across the pane: a thin film of frost, ice crystals forming geometric patterns on the window. As the flaming eyes fixed him, Chris saw his breath billow out white, felt a wave of bitter air, Arctic-icy, roll over him.

The chill of it seared through to his bones,

more so as more of the grey-faced shapes crowded closer to the window to stare at him. Chris flicked open his phone, thumbed the emergency services' number into it, but there was no ring, only that whispering static that had pervaded his dialogue with Julia, now grown deafening. Even so, he thought he heard whispers in it – voices, singing – before the phone went dead.

The back door. Chris ran to the kitchen – he could get out through there, run across the garden. Get over the wall, call for help. He pulled the cord, and the blinds that hung across the patio door drew back.

Four or five grey figures stood in his back garden; two moved closer to the doors, as if drawn by the thin candlelight. They didn't press up against the glass, stopping instead two or three feet from the doors, but the same wash of cold air blew over him as they approached.

Another appeared at the kitchen window. Its face was hunger and rage; irregular, luminous holes for eyes, and a torn stretched howl of a glowing mouth.

The song began as he stumbled back through into the living room. The one standing before the window had taken its hands from the glass; it, and the others outside, began to sway gently to and fro, from side to side.

The song droned on, and the chill in the room deepened. So did the sense of menace from the dull grey shapes. Chris couldn't make out the words they were singing: their voices were too thick and blurred, too toneless for him to be certain of the tune, but he thought the melody might be a much-corrupted version of a familiar carol, greatly slowed and slurred. The memories they evoked were so old and deep-rooted they were moods, ambiences, more than images or sounds – of warmth and safety, comfort and belonging. On the sofa between Mum and Dad, watching the Christmas Eve movie on television; in the church, half-asleep on a hard wooden pew, while the congregation rose, with a rumble of clothes, clatter of shoes on wood and sighing of breath, to sing:

And all the souls on Earth shall sing,
On Christmas Day, on Christmas Day,
And all the souls on Earth shall sing,
On Christmas Day in the morning,
Then let us all rejoice amain,

That was what those carols meant: a coming together. Love and goodwill to all. Worth hanging onto, surely, whether you believed or not? But this song was a discord, invoking those things only to reject them, a gleeful inversion of all the carol might mean – gleeful, if anything approaching glee could be connected to those yawning, yearning, craving faces of ash and dull fire. Would Julia be at the church now, the first sung notes echoing in the high ceiling? He should have gone. Why hadn't he? His reasons for not doing so seemed so trivial now. Let him get through this night unscathed and he'd act on his feelings for her; what was the risk of a little embarrassment if he realised he'd misread things? Nothing he couldn't survive.

The room was darkening.

Colder, colder, colder the living room grew. Breath blew white from him like smoke; teeth chattering, he dragged himself to the cupboard under the stairs, grabbed jackets and cardigans, a pair of gloves, and pulled them on. He went back one more time, to fumble thick-fingered in a crate of summer items and long-unused toys, where he found the string-wound handle of an old cricket bat and pulled it out. He felt the heft of it as he near-crawled back into the room.

As he reached the sofa, each breath scorching his throat, the candles' glow dwindled to yellow pinpoints; then one by one, the cold air pinched them out like fingers and thumbs, leaving only wisps of smoke and the dimming embers of wicks, and the only light came from the eyes and mouths of the faces pressed against the living room windows and patio doors, the glow rendered hazy, a nimbus, by the spreading patterns of frost.

The song droned on. The glow of mouths and eyes pulsed. And the cold grew bitterer still. They were drawing the heat from the room, the life from his blood.

After a while, the cold began to recede. He was starting to feel almost warm again. Hypothermia, he realised. He was in the church, the warm lights glowing around him, the warmth of Julia's shoulder a scant inch from his. She took his hand in hers. The choir sang, alleluia. Julia smiled at him: warmth, belonging, home. His head jerked, and he was in the living room again. The cold of it bit into him. There wasn't long left, not if he wanted to do something. Something like what? Why, escape of course. But how was that supposed to happen? They surrounded the house. They were many; he was one.

And if he tried to flee, and failed? What would happen to him, and how could it differ from what could happen if he stayed put?

Of course, this was cosier. Doing something, reaching out – those were always harder than staying put, doing nothing. They claimed more energy, took more effort, more courage. Hadn't that been why he'd stayed in tonight, instead of going to the church? He thought of Julia, her quiet warm-eyed face, the small well-lit house he'd only ever walked past, never seen the inside of but now so desperately wanted to. The little church only two streets away, where she'd be now. If he'd gone when she'd called, this wouldn't be happening. He was sure of that. They'd come for him, he was certain, because he'd been a target of opportunity – isolated, alone in the dark.

So as he pushed himself to his feet, leaning

on the cricket bat, he wondered if these things might not be the true 'reason for the season', after all. Was that why people gathered together on the long black nights, why they built lights and high fires; because they'd known that these waited in the dark for when the veils between the worlds grew thin, to seek out the stragglers, the friendless, the alone?

But he'd had a friend, and he'd turned away from her. He wanted to see Julia now; wanted that more than he'd wanted anything. To sit on a hard wooden pew and listen through the sermons and the lessons, to listen to the choir sing, and sing, and sing, holding back the darkness and the cold.

Pulling off a glove with his teeth. Fumbling in his pocket for the key to the patio doors. The song rising and falling, rising and falling.

The key in the lock – managing to insert it on the fourth or fifth attempt. The faces crowding close. The key turned; the tumblers clicked. Pushing the handle down.

Go out fighting. Fight and fight. On the offensive from the first second. Only chance you've got. He threw himself against the door and knocked it wide. Two of the grey things were flung backwards. Light as straw. He got both hands to the cricket bat's handle and went over the threshold as the others came at him. He swung once, hard, caught one of the grey things in the head. The eyes flickered and dimmed, and it fell sideways. He swung about him, left then right, clearing them back. Keep moving, don't stop. They had numbers, he had surprise and speed.

Another came at him; he swept the bat down in an overhead blow, the edge of it hitting the crown of its skull. A crunch, and the grey thing collapsed, pile-driven to the paving stones. The others backed up, circling. Their eyes and mouths pulsed and sang; still drawing the life from him.

He charged, swinging. Broke through. Running up the garden, hearing their whispering footfalls in pursuit. The bat in his hands, two charred patches bitten into either edge of it, one from each blow it had struck. Ignore that. Ignore them. He had to reach the wall, then clear it. A road ran parallel to the close – just a small side street, but it led to the main road, the city, to Julia. Surely they'd give up the pursuit then; surely creatures like these wouldn't dare be seen so openly, or they'd long ago have been exposed and destroyed.

The top of the wall was flat; he heaved the bat onto it and clambered up. As he did he saw they'd almost reached the wall; saw too, dismayingly, that the two he'd felled had risen to their feet and joined the pursuit.

Chris heaved himself on top of the wall as the first of the greys began to climb, hands and feet sticking to the brickwork; a lizard up a wall, or a spider. He grabbed the bat and struck down at its head, but lizard-quick its hand came free of the wall, flew up and grabbed the bat. The wood smouldered and blackened, the dark stain spreading out from around where the grey held it, then split and broke up, falling into ashes and char. The blackness crept down the handle, but instead of heat, it was cold that seared Chris's palm. He shouted at the pain, recoiled, and with another, louder, cry, he tipped back over the wall.

He landed on the bushes below; stripped bare by winter and turned hard and brittle by the cold, the branches speared him in a dozen places – one gouged his cheek, missing his eye by an inch – but they broke his fall and not his bones.

He scrambled to his feet, clothes torn, feeling blood run down his legs and arm and face, but feeling was returning – this cold was an honest winter's chill.

A fumbling above him; a grey hand groped over the wall, the top of a head, two dully glowing orange blobs. He broke into as much of a run as he could manage: he didn't have to get far, just to the end of the street and there'd be the city, there'd be people. But it was so quiet.

When he rounded the corner, he knew at once that something was wrong, but couldn't tell what. The city was dark, after all, but wouldn't it be? There was a power cut.

From behind there came soft, heavy thumps: his pursuers, coming over the wall. He broke into a limping run again, and as he did the city became more clearly visible. The buildings weren't just dark, but also empty. Shattered windows, ringed with soot; yawning doors; dust hardened into petrified mud on kerbs and pavements; wires of winter-blackened weed.

Abandoned, and not recently; and while they bore a passing resemblance to the buildings he passed every day, they were not the same. He was on their side of the mirror, not his own; he realised that just as the song began again behind him.

The cold gripped him immediately; he could almost see the warmth billowing out of his back in golden clouds to be sucked into those ravening faces. His vision blurred; had he seen a light, burning somewhere in the distance? Was it too late now to reach out? Please, let it not be too late. As the song grew louder he began running again; he stumbled blindly towards where he hoped the light might be, hoping he might find it, and perhaps others like himself, before his pursuers reached him.

It was near dark when Ace found the town of Pinner's Vale, breasting the tall pine-covered hill overlooking the low, mean huddled buildings and the winchtower of the mine. The sun was bled almost to extinction in the west, and the moon glowed ripe and thick and full.

Ace travelled light; he carried a switchblade in his coat pocket, the guitar he called Handsome Molly across his back in a polished red wood case, and a .45 automatic in his waistband. He didn't plan on advertising the last; New England was a long way from the Deep South, but white folks had little liking for a black man with a gun.

The mining town lay on the valley floor, in the crook of a winding stream that glittered like a silver wire. The slopes around it were thick with trackless pine woods like those Ace now wandered. On the opposite hillside stood a tall, wide building with soft-glowing windows. No miner's shack or factory building; this was a mansion.

A near-overgrown dirt trail wound down through the pines. Ace started down it; the dusk thickened round him as the trees closed in, crowding out the failing light. The pines formed a close, dark tunnel, but at least the sap made it smell fresh and sweet.

Then something growled, and a rank scent of animal breath washed out over him.

Ace went still. The thick woods were still wild – home to timber wolves, even bears. He let his hand fall slowly to the butt of the .45.

Red light gleamed in the dark; the undergrowth rustled and tore. Something came out to block his way.

Ace's first thought was *Bear*; the thing stood seven, eight feet tall. But the head was the wrong shape – too long – and the arms were like a man's arms, but with sharp curved claws on the fingers.

Ace backed away, tugging the .45 free and cocking it.

The beast stepped into moonlight, and Ace's stomach went hollow and cold. It had a man's body, though massively built and shaggily furred, but its head was a wolf's, long jaws hanging open and dripping drool, red light gleaming in the cores of its black eyes. A slow snarl escaped it; then it lunged.

For a second Ace was back in a trench in France, 1917, going hand-to-hand with the German soldiers. Old instinct took charge; he aimed two-handed, fired twice from the .45, the gun kicking up and back. The beast staggered, but its roar sounded more about anger than pain. It didn't even fall, just straightened up and snarled. Ace aimed between the red eyes and pulled the trigger.

The wolf's head snapped back, a muffled yelp escaping as the jaws snapped shut. It rocked back and thudded to the ground.

Then it snorted, shook its head, and got back up. Slowly, and looking *real* pissed off.

Ace felt his legs shake, and his arms too. He nearly dropped the .45. But he'd been a soldier, and you didn't forget, so when it charged he stood his ground and fired out the clip, hoping to run while the beast was down. But it barely even slowed, and lunged for him with a howl like knives on glass. A hand swiped at him and he threw himself down, hearing the whistle of its claws part the air as it went – but then the wolf-thing stood over him, drool spattering his face from its grid of curved teeth, blackened claws reaching down for him.

Then it jerked and spun – the rifle shot's flat crack came a second later, just as the wolf-thing howled. This time there was real agony in its cry, and maybe fear too.

Running footsteps, coming closer, then a voice:

"Stay on the ground! Stay where you are!"

Ace obeyed the first order but not the second; the beast had fallen uncomfortably close by and was laying about it in all directions with its claws. So he scrambled away, but kept low and near the ground, keeping the line of fire clear.

The wolf-thing thrashed about but didn't rise, its legs limp and unmoving, spine shattered, whining and snarling as clumped foam flew from its mouth.

A tall thin woman ran up. She wore rough hide trousers and a jerkin, a man's shirt underneath, and a band of cloth to hold the hair back from her eyes. She cocked the old Springfield rifle she held, snapping a brass shellcase from the breech, then threw it to her shoulder and fired.

Blood sprayed from the wolf-thing's head. Its snarls stopped and its body went limp. The woman jacked the bolt again. Then she turned, looked over at Ace. "Can you walk?"

He blinked. "Uh-huh."

"Then you might wanna. There's a whole lot more of these in the woods, and I ain't got bullets for alla them. Come on."

Shoving the empty .45 into his waistband and pausing only to check Molly was unharmed, Ace followed the tall woman down the hillside.

2

"Name's Eva," she said. "Eva Stillman."

"Ace Granchelet."

"Ace?"

"What folks call me."

Eva shrugged. She had long black hair and she was lean but handsome. Her skin was the kind of brown you weren't born with, but gained from a life outdoors in the wind and sun. "Brings you out here?" she asked.

"Came into Portland couple days back lookin' for work in the sawmills, but they weren't none goin'. Then I heard they needed men up at the silver mine in Pinner's Vale. That's here, ain't it?"

"Used to be," said Eva.

"What's it now?"

"Depends on who you ask."

"If I asked you?"

Eva glanced back at him. "I believe in what I see, mister," she said. "Which is werewolves. Same as you."

"Werewolves?"

"The hell else'd you call that thing back there?"

Truth was, Ace'd been doing his best to avoid giving it any thought. He'd seen war and a hundred kinds of cruelty and madness on his travels, before the Depression and since. Even a family of cannibals back in Georgia – which he did his best not to recollect – but this was something else.

Eva sighed, and for a second or so her face softened; she reached out and clapped his shoulder. "Come on. Need to get back over the river. Shouldn't be in the woods after dark."

"So why are you, ma'am?"

"Checkin' my traps. I'm the only one in Pinner's Vale ain't a miner. Lived out here with my daddy till he passed, couple years back. Taught me to hunt and trap. So you came out here lookin' for work? You don't much look like a miner."

"I been most things, one time or 'nother."

"Including a musician?"

Ace smiled. "Molly here ain't for decoration."

"Molly?" Eva chuckled, but stopped when she saw Ace's expression. "Easy, mister. No offence."

"I'm sorry. Hey..."

"What?"

"The hell you manage to kill that thing? I put a full clip in it."

"No mystery." Eva dug a bullet from a belt-pouch and flipped it to him.

"Silver?"

"Uh-huh. If you're gonna have werewolves on your hands, I'd say a silver mine's a good place to be."

"Lucky."

"Luck didn't have anything to do with it, mister."

Ace was about to ask her what she meant by that, but now they were clear of the woods, following a dirt-track to a bridge across the stream. As they crossed towards the low, mean houses huddled each side of the narrow street beyond, shadows moved out the darkness. People, he thought; but then he saw their faces.

3

"Jesus!"

Ace grabbed for the .45, forgetting it was empty, but Eva caught his wrist. "Easy, mister."

"Jesus," he said again. There were maybe a dozen people coming out to meet them. If *people* was the right term.

They were clothed, and they still had, to one degree or another, some of their humanity. Some.

Some had pointed ears, others pointed teeth, too large and too many to fit right in a human mouth. Their jaws wouldn't close properly, so saliva slicked their chins. Others still were dotted with tufts of thick, coarse hair. The woman leading the procession walked crooked, body buckled sideways by an arm grown massive and shaggy with fur, black, curved claw tips almost scraping the ground.

And in their eyes – in all their eyes, sooner or later – a glimmer of red light appeared.

"Easy, people," Eva called. "It's a friend."

Most of them just moaned. Maybe they were the only sounds they could make, or had the changes they'd gone through driven them mad? Most likely the second; Ace doubted a body *could* stay sane watching himself turn into a wolf like that.

The woman with the arm proved him wrong, though. Her face was tufted with hair and the teeth one side of her mouth were so distended there was blood as well as spit on her chin, but she spoke, and the words weren't so slurred Ace couldn't understand them.

"He here to help?"

A dozen pairs of eyes gleamed red at him. Ace swallowed hard and looked to Eva, but she just looked back. Then she grinned. "Might be. How 'bout you rustle up some stew, maybe a bottle of rye, and we can talk it over?"

After a moment, the woman nodded, but the tension didn't go and he could feel their eyes on him.

"And maybe a song or two," said Eva.

Ace smiled, at least till the first howl rang down from the hills above.

The first of many.

4

There was a saloon bar, next to the general store. Clapboard walls and bare-board floors strewed with sawdust, candles and hurricane lamps on the tables to give light. Ace sat one end of a table. The others sat lined up each side of it, all looking at him. It was a long damn table.

Still, singing for his supper suited Ace fine; it was the kind of work he best liked doing. He sang a few they'd know, like *Bullfrog Blues* and *Shake It And Break It*; then sang one of his own, *Middle Passage Blues*, which didn't go over half as well. Still, the others put smiles on the faces round him, and that was always good, whatever they looked like. Maybe, for just a little while, they forgot what'd been done to them.

The stew filled his belly and the rye warmed his blood. But in the end time came to put the guitar away.

"Was just me and my Daddy lived hereabouts till a couple years back," said Eva. "Then the company came and bought up the land. We lived up the hill, up in the pines, so they didn't bother us and we didn't bother them."

The mine had set to work and business was good – good enough that the miners and their families had fewer complaints than expected. And then John Valchin had come.

"John who?"

"Valchin," Eva said. "He's the big boss man, runs their company. Anyways, he's the one built the mansion up yonder. Word came down he was looking for something, in among the ore. Something meant a lot more to him than the silver."

"What?"

"The wolf's head," said the woman with the arm. "What he said he wanted. Said it'd be worked in some other kind of metal like pewter or lead, but buried in the silver. Promised a *big* bonus to whoever found it..." Her voice trailed off, choking up in her throat; her red-glinting eyes squeezed shut in pain.

"Lena here's husband—"

"I can tell it my own self!" Lena's still-human

hand hit the table top and the hurricane lamp jumped. Eva looked down. Quiet returned.

Ace started rolling a cigarette. When it was done, he offered it Lena. She licked her lips, blinked then shook her head. Ace lit up.

"My husband – he was the one found it. Had to fight off couple other men, tried to take it. Valchin'd promised ten thousand dollars to whoever brought it to him."

Ace blew out a stream of smoke and a thin whistle. Ten thousand would, most like, be pocket change to Valchin, but to a miner it'd be a king's ransom.

"Rodney said Valchin was like a kid with a new toy. Promised Rodney he'd have the money next day." Lena shook her head. "Don't know if'n he meant it or not, but either way we never saw it. That night he..." She shook, eyes wet and red. Ace held out the cigarette. Gratefully, she puffed it into life. "He changed," she said. Silence thickened the air in the saloon.

"Said he felt sick," she said, "went to lie down. I was fixing some coffee for him when I heard the... howl. Didn't hurt me." Her eyes brimmed and she shook her head. "But we had a little boy..."

Lena's voice strangled in her throat. She sat, head bowed, smoking down the last of the cigarette. Eva took over.

"Valchin played it down at first," she said. "Him and his men're the nearest thing to the law around here. Price – that was his head goon – put it round Rodney'd gone crazy, killed his son."

"Had a... private word... with Lena, too," said a bearded man with pointed ears and curved black claws for fingernails. "Said they'd lock her up in Danvers, she kept talkin' werewolves."

Someone refilled Ace's glass; he left it untouched. Wasn't no time for getting drunk. He didn't know what help there was – could be – for them, but they were hoping on something, and might cut up rusty they didn't get it.

"But then it started happening again," said Eva. "All 'cross the valley. There was better'n a hundred people in Pinner's Vale, maybe two." She gestured round the saloon. "This is all that's left."

"Jesus." Ace thought of the black, wooded hills he'd passed through. "You tellin' me there's two hundred werewolves runnin' loose?"

Eva nodded. "My momma was a Polack.

She'd spoke 'bout shit like this, back in the old country. Said they hate silver. So we made silver wire and put fencing round the town, keeps 'em out. But that's only half the problem. You can see the rest. Sooner or later, they all wind up hopping the fence and goin' up the hill to join the pack. Bum a smoke?"

Ace sighed, passed her the one he'd been rolling, started on another. "What about Valchin?" he asked. "He one of them too?"

Eva shook her head as she lit up. "Still up in his mansion," she said. "With some new goons. Ain't seen nothing of Price and his men in a long time now. But then we ain't seen much of any of the company men lately. They're up in the mansion with Valchin and that damn head, and we're down here."

"Thought of goin' up there?"

"Oh, we'd love to. Only trouble is—"

A chorus of howling cut her off. Everyone went still. Sobs hitched in throats; hands covered mouths. How many wolves howling? The whole two hundred? That was bad enough, but here it was more than a threat; it was the future too.

Eva took his hand. "Come with me."

Lighting up his cigarette at last, Ace followed her out onto the porch.

The night was clear, and the pines showed ghostly in the light of the moon and stars. But that wasn't the only light; a pale, icy beam shone from the mansion's upstairs window and swept across the serried ranks of pines. And wherever that strange light went, the wolves howled.

"Couple of times people tried to get out the valley," said Eva. "But wherever they shone that, the wolves came out. Like Valchin's got 'em trained, like you would a dog." Eva shook her head, looked down. "Nobody got out. 'Nother time we tried gettin' to the mansion, but they got guns." She patted the rifle. "I got this, and a .45 like yours. Countin' you in, that's three guns in Pinner's Vale ain't Valchin's. 'Sides which, no-one else here's in any shape to try bustin' in there to settle the bastard. 'Part from anything else, they're all so far gone whatever he's got up there could master them too. And on my own, I wouldn't stand a chance of getting in. But two people… were you in the army?"

So that's how it was. "France."

"They keep watch," she said. "Anyone tries to get out, they set the wolves on them." She picked a tobacco shred off her bottom lip. "Sides, there's something else you oughta know."

"What might that be?"

"Whatever happened, whatever Valchin did… spend any time here and it gets to you. We don't go in there, try and put a stop to it, you gonna be on the way to *that*." She pointed up at the hills. "Same as the rest of us."

"Don't seem to have marked you none."

Eva's smile vanished. "No?" She turned, pulled her shirt up over her bare back. All along Eva's spine rose a thick, coarse trail of grey-black fur. It was thickening across her shoulder-blades too.

She looked back over her shoulder and her eyes gleamed red. "Takes some slower than others. But takes us all in the end. So – you in or you out?"

5

Ace had two clips for the .45; he'd loaded both with silver bullets and put a fistful of loose rounds in each of his coat pockets. He ever made it out of Pinner's Vale, he could live for months on the leftover ammunition.

He had a hunting knife, too, sheathed at his hip. One of Eva's, with a silvered blade. The slopes beneath the mansion would be prowled by werewolves, and who knew what state Valchin or his guards were in? "Ain't no harm bein' careful," Eva said.

Ace grunted. Right now, he felt like the most outgunned man in the valley. He had the .45, Eva had her pistol and the rifle. Werewolves or no werewolves, there were better than a dozen armed men up there with Valchin, and it was a sure thing they'd have rifles, shotguns, maybe even a Thompson gun or two.

To even the odds a little, he and Eva both carried shoulder bags packed with straw. Each one held kerosene-filled bottles stuffed with torn rags. He didn't claim to know much about werewolves, but last he heard, fire killed most things.

The river running by the town circled the mine workings and then looped back along the foot of the hill where the mansion stood. There'd been a bridge there, but Valchin's men'd burned it.

"Think they'll know we're coming?" he asked.

"Uh-huh," Eva said. They looked at each other and both began to laugh, but it sounded wrong, too much like a scream. Ace knew it well, from France. It was the kind of laughter you heard before battle, with your whole damn body screaming *run* while your brain tried to tell it *no*. In France it'd been cos they shot you if you did. Here it was because he didn't have no choice. Climb the damn hill and fight, most likely die, but stand a chance of getting clear, or wait around with the others to become a wolf-man. Ace didn't need to flip a coin to pick. Some things were worse than dying; he'd seen an uncle of his die in the crazy-house.

"Alright," he said. "Let's move out."

~

Halfway across the stream, the bottom fell away. It wasn't the jolt of impact Ace minded so much as the cold hand that grabbed his balls as the water came up to his groin.

"Jesus!" He managed to keep it down to a hoarse whisper and kept on going. The .45 was in his fist, pointed skyward. The water didn't reach his waist, so his jacket pockets at least stayed dry.

Eva, moving ahead of him, rifle held above the surface, glanced back and gave a smile. Smile like that could drive you crazy, but there was something almost coy about it Ace liked. There was a lot to this woman. Maybe, this was over, they could...

Snap out of it, soldier. You got a job to do. Climb the damn hill 'fore you start thinkin' 'bout anythin' else. Can't dip your wick if you're dead.

The water got shallower towards the bank, thank God. Eva stayed on point; she knew the ground. She climbed through rushes, crouched on the bank, then motioned him to join her. Up above, the mansion's windows gleamed with lights.

"OK," whispered Eva. "Now it gets interestin'."

"Perfect," Ace whispered back.

The hope was to reach the mansion grounds without alerting Valchin's men, but knew it was a forlorn one. Only chance of that was a) not meeting any wolf-men along the way, which he already knew was about as likely as a chicken pecking rabbit turds and shitting gold, or b) killing any they *did* run into in silence. Only way of doing that was with a knife, and Ace wasn't *that* crazy. Eva had a blade on her hip had to be two feet long, but she'd already told him it was a last resort.

Still, at first, he'd call it easy going. He wouldn't've ordinarily; the ground was uneven, sloped up fast, but it beat the alternatives.

The whole front of the mansion was now in view. High walls enclosed the grounds. Eva'd said there were gardens, hothouses, sheds where they raised chickens and pigs, plus stores of canned and bottled goods. Valchin could wait out a siege in luxury. The only way in was a set of wrought-iron gates bound shut with heavy chains.

But they were almost there. *Shit, we might actually make it after all.*

Something growled in the dark up ahead. *Dumb bastard. Had to tempt fate.*

In the same instant, Eva slipped, falling. The rifle slid downslope, out of reach. Red eyes glowed up ahead and a thick, crouching bulk took shape.

"Shit," whispered Eva.

A snarl became a roar. The black bulk hurtled forward.

Ace fired; the roar became a howl. The black shape reared up, arms outflung. Ace fired again, and the howl cut off. The massive body crashed into the undergrowth. The wolf-man writhed about, steam billowing from its jaws and shattered chest, and let out a faint, piteous whine before it grew still. The red glow in its eyes fixed and faded.

Poor bastard. He could pity it now it was dead. It was a victim, same as Lena, Eva, all the rest. *You want to blame someone, blame Valchin. He's the one got to pay.*

Ace felt the shakes run down his arms. "Eva?"

She was down on all fours – he took a moment, even then, to appreciate the curve of her ass – picking up the rifle. "Yeah, I'm good... shit!"

Pale light flashed above then swept down, flaring through the undergrowth. *Searchlight?* But then there was howling from all about them. "Aw, *shit!*"

"What I said." Eva pulled back the rifle bolt. "We need to move."

Growls behind them. Ace opened his shoulder bag. "Light me."

Flame flickered in Eva's jittering hands. Ace couldn't blame her; his whole body felt like one big shake. Behind them, undergrowth rustled;

low growls and snarls sounded. They were coming from up ahead too; at the edge of his sight, their red eyes gleamed.

"Throw yours back down the trail," he whispered, as first one then the other rag fuse hissed into life. "I'll take care of what's up ahead." Eva nodded. "Now!"

Four or five wolf-men barrelled down the path and he threw his lit bottle. From behind him came a dull *whumph*, a yelp of triumph from Eva, and wolf-men howling higher than he'd thought them capable of. A bubble of flame erupted as Ace's Molotov hit, and there were more howls as the wolves scattered. All but two; one flailed about, its fur aflame, while the other hurtled on.

Calm. Ace breathed deep, let the moment stretch, aimed two-handed like he had all the time there was. Eva's rifle was firing behind him, but he barely noticed. He aimed square between the red eyes and pulled the trigger. Its head snapped back and it dropped. The burning werewolf had fallen and thrashed weakly on the ground. Ace walked closer, fired again. He covered his mouth against the smell of burnt hair and meat, trying not to gag.

"Come on!" Eva, scrambling past him. Above, pale light flashed about, waking howl on howl in a ragged chorus. How many more out there?

Behind us...

Ace spun and fired again, dropping a werewolf a second before its claws could find him, then leaping back as another closed. Two shots – he pulled the trigger twice and knocked the last pursuer flying backwards, slithering limp down the path.

Ace changed clips and ran after Eva toward the gate. There was a flash in a second floor window, then the angry stutter of gunfire, *rat-tat-tat, rat-tat-tat*, like stones raining on a tin roof. They crouched against the wall beside the gate.

"Thompson gun," Ace whispered.

The pale light swept through the woods below; howls answered it. Ace thumbed loose rounds into the emptied clip.

"We need to go," Eva said.

"I know." Four rounds loaded, five, six.

"Ace!"

"I know." Seven. "OK. How do we get in?"

"Only way in's the gate."

"Shit." Ace could see the chains from there,

links thick as his fingers. Even if he could pick them, they'd be in plain sight of Valchin's men. And the wolves were coming up the hill. "Then we need to climb the wall."

"They'll see us."

"Then we distract them."

They hurled the Molotovs as far over the wall as they could. Flame erupted and soared, and seconds later the Thompson gun began stuttering. "Go," said Ace, and they bolted past the gates to shin up the wall on the far side.

Eva went first, dropping into the grass. Ace was straddling the wall when a shot whistled by his ear and another chipped brickwork inches from his nose. The Thompson gun stuttered again, muzzle flashing. Eva, in the grass, aimed up and fired. The Thompson's stutter cut out; a moment later, a headless body toppled through the window, still clutching it.

"Roland!" someone in the house screamed.

Eva was already up and running. Ace jumped, knees bent, rolled and rose, putting a hand to his shoulder bag to ensure his remaining bottle hadn't broken.

Eva was running in a straight line; Ace yelled at her to weave. She looked back, saw him zigzagging side to side, and did the same. Another bullet sang past Ace's head, then another – this time the muzzle flash was in a downstairs window. Ace fired two shots at it and no more were fired back at him.

The headless Thompson gunner lay near the front door; Ace grabbed the submachine gun and a spare clip from the body. The downstairs window was shattered and the thick floor carpet in the room beyond was slowly turning red around the body of a suited man with a rifle in his hands.

"Nice shot," Eva crouched, rifle shouldered.

"Thank you."

"Now how 'bout getting us in?"

Ace tried the front door. "Locked."

"No shit?"

Ace sighed, then shot the lock out with the Thompson and kicked the main door wide.

6

The door opened on a fancy hallway – thick pile carpet, paintings on the wall, some of them downright indecent (leastways, that's what Ace's father would've said) and a chandelier hanging from the ceiling. A flight of wood-panelled stairs topped with a solid brass rail led upwards.

And down in the valley they're scratching for a livin' and turnin' into dogs.

Two men running down the hall, both armed. Ace cut down on them with the Thompson and they spun and fell. *Fast, no time to think about it. Think later, if you think at all. Once a soldier, always a soldier.* Eva's rifle cracked; a body crashed down the staircase.

The shot man lay coughing blood. Ace stood over him, pointed the Thompson at his face. "Valchin. Where?"

Eva covered the hallway while the man coughed and spluttered blood. *"Where?"* Ace heard his voice come out in a growl, wondered if his eyes gleamed red, the change already starting. "Where's Valchin?"

The man spat blood and managed to speak. "Observatory. Upstairs. Top floor..." Then his head rolled back and his eyes fixed, glazing already. Ace felt the urge to close them, but there wasn't time. Instead he nodded briefly to himself, then turned to Eva. "Come on."

He lit up his remaining Molotov and pitched

it down the hallway. Fire raced across the carpet, up the walls. "Should keep 'em occupied," he told her, and bounded up the stairs, trying to guess how many shots were left in the Thompson.

Two things happened when he reached the mini-landing halfway up; Eva yelled his name and he saw two men on the landing above, one racking a shotgun. He leapt back and the blast ripped hell out of the panelling he'd been stood in front of. The gunman racked the slide again; the second aimed a heavy revolver. Ace fired the Thompson up the stairs. The first man pitched backwards and the shotgun fired up, blowing out the chandelier; the second man dropped to his knees and slumped forward, slithering head-first down the staircase. The Thompson emptied, the barrel smoking. Ace replaced the empty drum-clip and started on up again.

Four floors, with Valchin at the top. Ace peered up the next flight. "Looks clear. Go on up. I'll cover you."

Eva went up. The only sound was the crackle of flames and the howling of the wolves outside. Smoke caught the back of his throat. Getting out of here would be a bitch, but that could wait. He'd made it out of worse. First thing was to find

Valchin, else he wanted to wind up howling at the moon and eating his meals raw.

"All clear," Eva called.

Ace climbed to the foot of the last flight. The lights were out. In the dark above that weird pale light flickered. Ace put a foot on the first riser. A low growling rolled out the dark. The pale light flashed towards him and backlit two shapes at the top of the stairs. Red eyes glowed.

"Kill them!" called a voice from the dark. "Kill them both!"

One of the werewolves vaulted the banister, dropping to the flight below. *Eva!* Ace opened his mouth to yell a warning, but then the second werewolf hurled itself down the stairs at him.

Ace fired, knocking it back and down, but it thrashed and flailed, howling as its claws hacked divots out the stair carpet and trying to climb back up even as the bullets hit it.

They ain't silver bullets. Just lead.

Course not. If Valchin controlled the werewolves, silver bullets would be an extravagance, and maybe give his men ideas.

Ace dumped the Thompson and drew the .45, but then the thing was on him and the gun went flying. He heard himself screaming. Its claws on its shoulders. The jaws gaped. A foul wind of breath gusted out. Hot.

The hunting knife – he found and pulled it free. The fanged muzzle lunged for his throat. Ace punched out with his knife hand. A howl gurgled and died; the werewolf stumbled back, the knife-hilt sticking out of its throat, then toppled back down the stairs.

"You OK?"

Ace looked down to see Eva wrenching the knife from the dead beast's throat. The other wolf lay dead behind her. She handed him back the knife and reloaded her rifle. These had been her neighbours, maybe even friends, Ace realised for the first time, to say nothing of her potential future, but if killing them troubled her a whit she gave no sign of it. A hard woman. To be admired, but maybe feared too.

Ace cleaned and sheathed the knife, picked up the .45. From the dark above there was only silence, waiting and expectant.

"Ready?" Eva whispered.

Ace nodded.

"Then let's finish this."

Together, they climbed the stairs.

A thin figure hunched over something on a swivel-stand, jerking it frantically back and forth. Pale light flashed from it out the casement windows.

"Don't move." Ace aimed the .45; Eva crouched and shouldered the Springfield.

The figure went still. Ace saw its eyes glisten as it stared at them.

"Step away from that thing. Where's the lights?" When he got no answer, Ace walked to the man and caught his collar as he tried to duck away. "I asked you a question, mister."

"There." The man pointed.

"Eva, go check."

"Yes, massa," she called back, bitter laughter in her voice. Ace smiled too, whether she saw it or not.

A click, then cold light, flaring on. Electric; Ace narrowed his eyes against it, gripped the man's collar tighter and shoved the .45 to his head.

Eva came back. "Valchin."

Ace inspected their catch. Younger than he'd expected. Maybe twenty-six. Dark hair in a wide, floppy fringe almost to his eyes, which were wide and pale-blue. His thin, white face was pretty, almost girlish. He looked like someone who'd always got what he wanted, whatever it was, without delay. He wore a fancy suit with a yellow cravat, but it was dirty and stained.

Eva dragged up a chair. Ace looked around; far as he could see, the whole top floor was one big room, half-library and half-museum. Charts and tapestries hung from the walls, showing strange diagrams. There were statuettes and carvings, all of them showing wolves of one kind or another. And there were twisted, dried things, and things in bottles, and Ace didn't like looking at none of them. And there was the thing on the stand; a mirror of black polished crystal in a silver frame. The top of the frame was a snarling wolf's head with rubies for its slitted eyes.

"It's the Mirror of Azralek," said Valchin. His voice, Ace figured, had to be one of the ugliest sounds he thought he'd ever heard. High and quavering, like it'd never quite broken – one moment it'd sound almost senile, like some mean old man who'd forgot damn near everything except malice, and the next like a spoilt, petulant kid. Bad enough in itself, but add it to the smooth, pretty face and soiled dandy's outfit and something about it made even touching Valchin hateful. Ace was glad to shove him in the chair. Valchin winced but kept on talking. "It gives the wielder the power of control over the—"

"Yeah," said Ace. "We saw."

"There," said Eva.

On a table near the window was a silver cage. Inside it, a life-size wolf's head, crudely-worked in lead or maybe pewter. "That's what this is all about?"

"Uh-huh."

"Where's it from?"

Valchin smiled. "Somewhere old. The precise origins are obscure. Von Junzt suggests—"

"Shut up."

"It contains a… power," said Valchin, quickly. "For want of a better word. When controlled, it can accomplish great things. Wonders."

Flames crackled and the wolves howled in the woods. Smoke stung Ace's eyes and caught his throat. "Yeah. I seen some of your wonders already."

"No, you don't understand. That was an

accident. The ancients buried it here because the earth is rich with silver, which nullifies the power. When it was taken out of the ore, the power was released. The effects didn't reach any further than this valley – they might have, in time, but then we put it in the cage, you see. The cage is silver. So it's controlled. Contained."

"Controlled?" snarled Eva. "You seen what it's done down there?" Red light glinted in her eyes. Ace put a hand on her arm.

"They're only miners." Valchin was either mad, Ace decided, or so used to buying his way out of trouble he'd lost all sense of danger. "They're replaceable. The results we're achieving here justify a few unfortunate side-effects."

"So it was never about the silver," said Eva. She sounded very calm, which maybe made Valchin think she wasn't angry anymore. *Jesus. You really have no idea, do you?* Ace found himself staring at Valchin as he would've at a dead werewolf, given leisure to do so. Some member of a species very far from anything he could understand.

"Of course not. Oh, I had to act as if it was – Dad would never have given me the money I needed if I'd told him the real reason. I'd found the ancient documents showing where the head was buried, and I knew that would mean silver. So I had the perfect cover – it gave me all the backing I needed to search for the head, and it actually made some money to keep my stupid old Dad happy." He giggled like a child. "And as long as the silver kept coming, he couldn't care less what goes on out here."

"And what exactly did you plan on doing with this... power?" said Eva.

Valchin blinked.

"Well... I don't know, really. Hadn't thought that far ahead. I mean, the applications are..." he faltered. "I just wanted to prove I wasn't a fool. Show Dad I wasn't the 'useless waste' he kept calling me." The voice had gone sullen and petulant. "But just think! Can you imagine how this will revolutionise how we view the world—"

Click. The rifle bolt snapped back. Eva's face was almost white. "Can *you* imagine," she asked, voice shaking, "how this will revolutionise your fucking brains?" Her finger tightened on the trigger. Valchin mewled and a foul stink filled the room.

"Wait." Ace caught her gun-arm. "We ain't done with him yet."

"You heard him. Did you hear him? He did this to us, and it was all for what? Just so this limpdicked bastard could impress his Daddy? That's worth our lives to him. That's worth our goddamn *lives*."

"I know, but we ain't done with him, Eva. Remember what we came for." Ace put his face close to Valchin's. "How do we put right what you've done?"

"You can't."

Ace put the .45 under Valchin's chin. "Wrong answer, white boy. You might wanna try again." He was shaking; the terror of the wolf was on him now, teeth seeking his throat.

"It can't be taken back. The one thing the wolf's head can't do is reverse the effects of the uncontrolled power. It's like electricity. It can do a great deal, but it can't bring back a man killed in the electric chair. Do you see?" He studied Eva. "Some change faster than others. But I'm sorry – I'm truly sorry." The voice was panicked and whimpering and the smell'd got worse. "Once it's started it can't be stopped. I'm sorry. I'm sorry."

"So am I." Ace cocked the .45. Valchin squealed.

"Wait! Wait! You only came here tonight, didn't you? Then you're safe! Don't you see? The wolf's head was shielded by then. Contained. Price and the others who were with me at the time – they changed too. They're in the woods with the others. So I sent for replacements... they've been here ever since, and they're unharmed."

"Not anymore," Ace pointed out.

"But you been here from the start," said Eva, "and you ain't changing. So there's a way. So quit your lying and tell me the truth."

"I'm not lying!" Valchin fumbled with a thick gold chain around his neck, pulling a square amulet into sight. "The Shield of Azralek. It protects the owner from the power. It was never able to affect me in the first place. But once it's begun..."

Eva sagged, then started coughing. Smoke was pouring into the observatory. Ace went over to one of the far windows. "We need to get outta here. Get this window open, we could get away 'cross the roof..."

Eva didn't answer, but Valchin started screaming. "No! No! Please" The last word was a shrill, hysterical screech. Ace turned to see Eva forcing Valchin's face against the bars of the silver cage with one hand, trying to open it with the other. The amulet lay on the floor.

Ace ran over. "Get away from there."

"Like hell. What you going soft on him for?"

Ace pointed the .45 at her head.

"What the hell you doing?"

"Let go that cage."

"It's what he deserves," she yelled back.

"You open the cage and I go too. That ain't happenin'."

Eva blinked, calming a little. Then she nodded down at the floor where the Shield of Azralek lay. "Then put that thing on."

8

Dawn; a light mist rolled through the valley, blending with the pale, itchy smoke lifting from the blackened ruins on the hillside.

Eva walked back from the old mine workings, the other villagers trailing behind her, but one by one they drifted off, till the street was empty save for her, Ace and the naked, whimpering figure tethered to a stake outside the general store.

"Guess I ain't so popular," said Ace.

Eva snorted. "Me neither. Ain't your fault. They were all hoping we could stop it."

Ace nodded. "You buried it?"

Eva nodded. "Deep in the mine. Get dynamite later, bring it all down." She nodded over at the naked figure by the general store. Even from there, Ace could see where the first tufts of coarse fur had sprouted. "Valchin's changin' already. Like Lena's husband – he was right next to the head."

"So were you."

She shrugged. "Don't feel no different. Guess it touches you once, it don't want to do it again. Suits me fine. Ain't complainin'. Any luck, he'll be a wolf long before I am. So I can watch him go crazy with fear, watch him suffer and beg. And when the last little bit of whatever makes him a man's about to go outta him, *that's* when I got a silver bullet with his name on it." She sighed and rumpled up her black hair with long thin fingers. "Ain't much, but it's somethin'."

Ace nodded. "Don't make you feel no better, but 'least you can feel you balanced the books a little, huh?"

"Yeah. Whatever good that is."

Ace didn't know either, so he changed the subject. "What'll you do once Valchin's gone?"

She shook her head. "Ain't been thinking that far 'head. Do what I can for the others. Then… well, there ain't but two choices, are there? Live as a wolf or die as a woman. I got a while to choose. Either way, I wouldn't come back this way to look me up."

Ace laughed, though he didn't feel much like it. "You ain't *that* special."

"No?" She eyed him, head cocked, a buckled sort of smile on her long brown face, then caught hold of him and put her lips on his, tongue darting round in his mouth, then pushed him away. "Still think so?"

Ace blew out a long breath. "You're something."

"I know."

"I'm… sorry."

"Like I said, ain't your fault. Thanks for doing what you could."

There was nothing more to say. Ace spared Valchin a last glance. The man's face mingled terror and disbelief. *Finally found something you can't buy your way out of.* They'd come looking, but whatever they found, they wouldn't find him. Or Eva. Or, most probably, anyone else.

"So long, Eva." He couldn't say *take care*, or *be well*, because she couldn't do either. She nodded.

"Safe journey, Ace."

9

He climbed the woods above Pinner's Vale again, gun in his belt, this time loaded with ammunition that'd keep him safe. Just in case, although the wolves tended to sleep by day.

The undergrowth rustled and he spun. A hulking figure crouched by the path, human-shaped but shaggy with fur and bearing a long wolf's head.

Ace looked into its black, red-cored eyes and was still, pondering a grab for the .45, but the werewolf made no move towards him. From the undergrowth came a low whining; two smaller versions of the creature huddled against its flanks.

After the longest of moments, Ace lifted and spread his hands.

The creatures remained still.

Ace moved slowly off. They made no move.

Finally, the mother turned, led her cubs off into the pines.

Ace kept walking.

10

Soon enough there was a town, and soon enough a station, and then soon enough a freight train. Ace snuck aboard one of the cars. There were a couple hobos there already. Both were white. They said nothing to him, and he sat at the far end of the car. Could be they didn't like Negroes, or maybe they just weren't the sociable type. Ace didn't feel too sociable himself, that was fine by him.

He took Molly out of her case, though, laid her on his lap and began to play as the train started rolling. The air was getting cold; soon it'd be winter in America.

After a while, one of the hobos took out a mouth harp and started to play along with him. In such a manner, they became companions for a time. And Ace Granchelet played a slow, sad melody on the guitar called Handsome Molly, for a dark-eyed, fierce-kissing woman by the name of Eva Stillman.

I spent Christmas 2005 with Dad; my first since leaving home. In the past I'd only come for a day; this time I'd come up Christmas Eve, leaving the morning of the 27th. Not that long a stay, but long enough. For all the vitality he displayed, his remaining hair was grey, face lined. Liver spots on his hands. He moved stiffly at times – he was ageing. I realised, the way you realise an obvious truth, that there were only so many opportunities left to spend time with him. So he found it easy to extract a promise to visit later in the New Year. "Come up May or thereabouts," he said.

I booked off the week of the May Bank Holiday, took the train to the nearest town and the bus to Redburgh; Dad met me at the station. We hugged awkwardly; he insisted on taking my bags and loading them into his battered car. "How are you, anyway, Paul?" he asked me.

"I'm OK." I told him the kind of things I hoped would keep him happy – a good job, well-paid. It would've pleased Mum, anyway. What he hoped or expected, I no longer knew.

~

Redburgh was far enough up along the Fylde coastline that Blackpool was reduced to a blurred, lurid stain in the distance, which was the best thing for it far as I was concerned. A shingle beach was bracketed by a jetty one side and the old harbour, long since silted up, on the other. Behind the village were two low hills, green splashed with purple heather and yellow gorse, marred only by the abandoned factory midway up the slope of one. It was recessed into a deep combe, as if sunk in to the hillside.

Dad had bought up an old workers' cottage at the foot of the hill in question following the divorce – long enough before the housing boom to be able to afford it. There was even a small stream running through the unkempt vegetable garden.

We stepped onto the small patio out back so I

could see it properly. I'd glimpsed it before, but winter's never the best time to view such places. Dad chuckled. "Not bad, eh?"

"No. Not at all."

We sat up late talking over anything and nothing, steadily putting away most of a bottle of Bushmills in the process. It was our first real conversation – one where we were two people, not father and son. No struggles for dominance or independence. To our mutual surprise, perhaps, we basically liked what we found.

Around midnight, he took out his old guitar, despite my protestations, and began to play softly. I stopped protesting after a while. I heard some traditional folk tunes, a couple of blues numbers, and a few others that seemed neither nor, and might have been his own. He wouldn't say. Now and again he'd sing. His voice had been something once; too much in the way of cigarettes and whisky had cracked and faded it. He talked a little while he played, but his mind wasn't really on it. His eyes kept stealing away from me, up towards a pale, blurred light, high up on the hill.

~

Around one, he stopped playing, laid the guitar aside. "Old habit," he apologised. "I never sleep till late, so I always play midnight till one."

I frowned. "Why?"

He shrugged. "Just something I do. Keeps me in practice."

Dad'd been in a band in the late seventies. I wasn't exactly sure what their music might've been called, but I'd liked the odd snippets I'd heard. One independently pressed EP; four songs to hold against the dark, played each time through a thicker layer of crackle.

"It was the end of something," he said, "the end of the seventies. Young people'd had something till then. Mind of their own. A culture of their own. Music of their own, the stuff that'd get in the charts. Folk, prog-rock, punk, you know, whatever – we found it ourselves, made it ourselves, it was ours. And after that time, no. It was just the crap they spoon-fed you. What to listen to, what to think." He frowned, shaking his head, trying to define it to his own satisfaction. "It was like in 1979, all of that turned to glass..."

For a second he went still, looking down at the floor, licking his lips. "Glass," he said again.

"Glass... anyway." He shook his head. "We came here, once, you know. The band, I mean."

"To Redburgh?"

"Mm." He dug a snapshot out of his wallet. Faded and embarrassing in terms of dress sense and hairstyles, but he looked good in that. Like me, but with longer hair. Strange to see a face so like your own, knowing it's not yours. He'd been one of two guitarist-cum-vocalists; the other had long hair and a droopy moustache. Mind you, that could've described any of the band. They were on the beach, the jetty in the background. I returned the photo.

"We came up here in '78," he said. "You'd've been four or five. Stayed in a B&B. Your Mum took that picture..." He chewed the corner of his mouth. "We broke up not long after that – the band, I mean." He and Mum'd stayed together for years; they'd waited till I left home.

He fell silent. I looked up at the hill; the pale light had gone. I took that as my cue.

Later, drifting off to sleep, I heard his guitar again.

~

I went hiking the following day – I'd already strolled through the streets of Redburgh, gone up and down the jetty, crossed the beach, gazed out to sea and pottered round the harbour, which'd pretty well exhausted all other possibilities inherent in the town. The view from the hills was more extensive – I could see several miles up the coast in both directions, out to sea and inland.

It was a warm, bright afternoon, more like July than May, and so the sunset caught me by surprise. I didn't know the hills well enough to risk them in the dark, so I turned back.

About ten minutes from the foot of the hill, I passed the abandoned factory. It was a square, heavy, red brick box with twin chimneys, clutched by ivy and flanked by thickets of pale silver birch. Most of its windows were broken. Dying light caught on them, orange and red.

Due to the angle, the side nearest me didn't really catch any of the sun; if it had the glow wouldn't have been noticeable, the reflection off the windows would've covered it. But I did see it; an odd, pale light that blinked as it moved between windows, flickering like the lambent flame of a Bunsen burner as I looked up at it. I took a step in its general direction. Then suddenly it waned and... went out? Or did it move away?

I had a brief yen to explore the factory – abandoned buildings are an old fascination for me – but the sun had slipped that bit lower and the broken windows no longer gleamed. It just looked dulled and unsafe, and somehow expectant. The dimmer the light got, the more a sense of threat seemed to gather about it. I almost broke into a run, back down to the road and finally the little lane where, in the back garden of his cottage, Dad was plucking old tunes out on his guitar.

~

For someone who'd long given up any idea of being a musician, my dad seemed to spend an awful lot of time playing music.

This occurred to me a couple of days later, towards the end of my week in Redburgh. Thinking back to my Christmas with him, I'd often retired early, the sea air robbing me of my usual insomnia (normally I was most definitely a night-owl, as was he; perhaps it was something in the Hearn genes) only to be lulled to sleep by the gentle strumming, plucking or picking of his guitar. When I mentioned it he just said "Well, I knew in the end I wasn't going to make a living off it, so I stopped trying to. But I always enjoyed it – still do."

I had no answer to that. But I woke up in the early hours of the morning and realised he was still playing. *Not just midnight till one*, I thought. Was he that obsessed with it, the need that great? I wandered through into the kitchen and saw him through the patio doors. He was sitting in the garden, playing, and staring up. Up towards the hill, and a pale blur of moving light.

~

I went back to bed that night without alerting him to my presence; towards the end of the following afternoon I was back up in the hills again. I didn't admit to any curiosity about the pale light; it just meant that as the dusk approached I happened to be standing near the old factory, watching again as its windows blazed and glowed, then died like embers. I mulled going in or not. Curiosity versus that undefined sense of threat. I knew enough, by now, not to dismiss such feelings out of hand.

All the same, I found myself walking towards it. I climbed the fence surrounding the factory and its combe, and started through waist high grass towards it.

The old gravel drive was hopelessly overgrown. Roots broke the surface; I stepped over them and walked. I walked under the rusted framework of the factory gates, and headed for the main door.

~

The interior was dim. Soft, faint sounds; dripping noises, the faint rustle and slither of things in motion.

I wished I'd brought a torch, then remembered that I had. A small pocket job I'd picked up walking in Redburgh earlier. I'd no idea why, at the time – or at least none that I'd admit to.

I shone the beam around and moved forward. Paint peeled from brickwork; old pipes and machinery had rusted solid. The light gleamed off something. Ice. Ice in May. I went closer, shone the torch on it. A handprint in ice, still clinging to the wall. Inside it, the light caught and glittered in patterns; patterns that appeared to be made by the lines and whorls you'd find on any hand, or fingers.

Only it wasn't just a print. There was part of the hand itself. Or a cast of it made in ice, at any rate. I saw a fingertip, a whole fingertip, perfect in detail right down to the ragged nail. I peered closer and realised, *wrong again*. It wasn't a cast; the fingertip was solid. And then I realised the most obvious mistake. It wasn't ice; it was glass.

The floor glittered too. I shone the torch down. Fused to the floor were two boot prints in glass.

There was a flicker of luminescence to my left; I spun round, the torch-beam flashing up a flight of steps that bent round leading to the next level of the factory. A pale glow flickered from around the corner, then was gone.

I started up the stairs.

~

When I stepped out onto the floor above and shone my torch around, its beam broke into a million splinters that were flung back at me.

Glass was on the broken walls, the floors and the ceilings; columns of it came down, stalagmites and stalactites. It coated the rusted machinery like molten toffee, and like toffee it'd been pulled and stretched into new shapes, creating a three dimensional web, a glass maze.

I heard something moving. Something big. I heard a hissing, like a snake. Dancing all about me in the warped and broken glass, I saw splinters of another light, a pale one that had nothing to do with my torch.

The light stole into the shapes of the glassy surface, the bumps and the hollows that formed faces, or seemed to. It filled them out and I thought I saw faces I recognised, familiar ones; faces, I thought, from the snapshot my father had showed me.

As the source of the pale luminescence began to flop and slither through the glass web, the labyrinth of glass, I heard sounds, ringing out from the glass where it was touched. It sounded like notes of music; stolen music no-one would ever hear, except those drawn in here, to join its makers.

I glimpsed a manlike figure pressed flat against the wall; for a moment I thought I'd found a fellow sufferer, but then saw he was all of glass as well and long past any help I might give, save to smash him to dust with a hammer.

Every detail of him was, or had been, perfect; his left arm had been flattened into a vitrified smear that had then been wound and teased out – the glass must at stages have been rendered liquid, like cooling toffee – to be smoothed into the labyrinth of stolen song that occupied the room. One side of his face was being smeared – in slow stages, by the look of it – into his left shoulder and arm. I wondered when he'd been lured in. When, and how, the others in the band had been. And how my father had escaped.

The glow flickered from all around me. Whichever way I turned, I might see. That was what made this place the perfect trap. You never knew which direction *not* to look in.

It was close. A rush of warm rank breath brushed the back of my neck.

That was when the web began to sing again. A different tune. It hummed, whined, got louder. The different songs blurred into a single note, then became a melody, an oddly familiar one. Something hissed, and the breath was gone from my neck. The pale light receded; the glitter of the web dimmed. Soon it was dark once more, and the web ceased to sing. After that there was only the faint sound of an old guitar playing in the distance, at the foot of the hill, some old blues or folk song, or another kind, a kind you couldn't quite define.

~

When I made it back home, I had dinner with my father and we repeated the other rituals we'd built up during our stay. He said nothing about the factory and I didn't feel able to broach the subject, so I've no idea if he knew what'd happened, or if it was just plain luck that he played when he did. Perhaps he just played whenever he saw the light out there.

We didn't discuss it, or what'd happened to the band, whether the thing in the factory had taken them all at once, only dad escaping – if it is an escape when you come back to the place and remain there, playing forever – or if it had lured them back, one by one, year after year.

If nothing else though, perhaps there's some explanation for why my life seems to have become a magnet for the darkness, for the strange. Perhaps it's just in the blood.

I left the next morning; Dad drove me to the station. "Will you be all right?" I asked as I boarded the bus.

He just smiled. "I'll be OK," he said. "I'll just keep on keeping on."

As ever, we struggled to communicate; the bridges we'd rebuilt could only achieve so much. Other areas were, as ever, sealed off. But as the coach pulled out, I watched him walk away and realised that at last my father was someone I could live up to: keeping on keeping on, and singing back the dark.

-For Joel Lane.

Ghost Notes

In music, a 'ghost note' – also known as a dead or muted note – is a note played solely for rhythm, with no discernible pitch. It doesn't form part of the melody, but still adds to the tune as a whole. Likewise, you don't need to read these notes to enjoy the stories – I wouldn't be doing my job properly if you did – but if, like me, you're one of those people who enjoys hearing writers talk about how the magic's made, they might still add something. If you're *not* one of those people, then no biggie, you can skip them if you like. But before you go, please accept my gratitude for parting with your hard-earned cash to buy a copy of *Singing Back The Dark*. It means a lot. (And if you haven't read the stories yet, then stop reading this now and do that before you read these! Otherwise I'll set a werewolf on you.)

The Psalm was inspired by driving across Saddleworth Moor on a rainy October afternoon. The bleak, atmospheric setting was just crying out for a suitably eerie and unsettling story; the title (as often happens) had been waiting around in my notebooks for a suitable tale, and one night I sat down and wrote the piece in a single, pretty painless session. It's similar to an earlier story, *The Climb*, in showing a recently bereft man hounded across some part of the Lancashire landscape by a largely unseen menace, but I think the two are different enough that no-one should feel short-changed.

Hard Time Killing Floor Blues owes a lot to the many Monday nights I spent at Swinton Folk Club in the mid-2000s, usually getting pleasantly buzzed on Black Bush whiskey. The club was home to an eclectic mix of musicians, among them two outstanding bluesmen, Pete Ryder and Dai Thomas. Dai played Appalachian folk songs and classic Mississippi Delta Blues (still does, as far as I know), which was how I got to hear songs such as *Last Kind Word Blues*, *Handsome Molly*, and, of course, Skip James' *Hard Time Killing Floor Blues*.

There was no way titles like that couldn't inspire a writer, and one morning after a night out at the club, the name 'Ace Granchelet' popped into my head. I still have no idea where it came from, but the concept of a bluesman wandering Depression-era America and battling evil and monstrous things in between songs came along with it shortly after. I can't quite remember how much of *Hard Time Killing Floor Blues* had been worked out in advance before I set to work, but I do remember the whole story pretty much writing itself in one marathon all-night session that finished in the small hours, sustained by vast amounts of coffee.

And All The Souls In Hell Shall Sing started with the title. No idea where it came from, but it got added to the long list of Possible Story Titles I periodically update and I thought it had a nice ring. Obviously it needed to be set around Christmas, at which point I remembered reading that the suicide rate always spikes up during the holiday because so many people are alone – easy prey to loneliness and depression. And, in this case, to worse things still.

Moon Going Down was Ace Granchelet's second outing, written nearly a year after *Hard Time Killing Floor Blues*. This time I decided the threat needed to be supernatural in nature, as the monsters in the first story had been only too human. Ace was going to be facing menaces of every kind as his travels across America continued.

The metal wolf's head pops up in a couple of other stories, *Salvaje* (which appeared in *The Ninth Black Book Of Horror*) and *Kiss The Wolf* (published in Conrad Williams' debut anthology *Gutshot*), both of which feature another would-be series character of mine called Luisa Bardillo.

There were to have been a whole series of stories about Ace – apart from anything else, there were so many more blues song titles crying out to be used (*Hellhound On My Trail*, *Death Letter Blues* and *When Lightning Struck The Pine* are just a few of them) – and about Luisa too. Gary McMahon urged me to write an Ace Granchelet novel, but it never quite happened. I've made a few attempts at writing series characters and never managed to sustain it as I wanted. Maybe I will one day, and maybe Ace Granchelet will ride the rails again.

As a side note, I had fun salting the story with musical references, just for fun. There's a traditional blues/folk song, a Bruce Springsteen song, one by Warren Zevon and one by Gil Scott-Heron. You can amuse yourself looking for them if you like. Call it a hidden extra.

Effigies Of Glass was the last in another would-be story cycle, this time about reluctant/accidental psychic detective Paul Hearn. I wrote seven stories about Paul between 2005 and 2007. Three others have seen print: *Hushabye* appeared in Ellen Datlow's anthology *Inferno*, and was reprinted in her anthology *Nightmares: A Decade Of Modern Horror*, *Winter's End* appeared in the Gray Friar Press anthology *Home Is Where The Heart Is*, and *The Battering Stone* appeared in the anti-austerity horror anthology *Horror Uncut*. *Horror Uncut* was the brainchild of Tom Johnstone and the late Joel Lane; Joel's own series of 'weird police' stories, as collected in his book *Where Furnaces Burn*, were a major inspiration for the Paul Hearn tales. He enjoyed the stories, and *Effigies Of Glass* most of all.

The title had been hanging around in my notebooks for a while by then, but Joel actually uttered the line about how the youth culture of the '60s and '70s 'turned to glass' during a telephone conversation, and so the story was born. When I mentioned it to him he was pleasantly surprised to have come up with the image, having completely forgotten the original comment. So in more ways than one *Effigies Of Glass* owes a lot to Joel's influence as a writer and as a friend. That's why it was, and remains, dedicated to him.

Simon Bestwick
Wallasey
October 2018

Also by Simon Bestwick:

Novels

Tide of Souls (Abbadon Books, 2009)

The Faceless (Solaris, 2012)

Black Mountain (Spectral Press, 2014)

Hell's Ditch (SnowBooks, 2015)

The Feast of All Souls (Solaris, 2016)

Devil's Highway (SnowBooks, 2016)

Wolf's Hill (SnowBooks, 2018)

Collections

A Hazy Shade of Winter (Ash Tree Press, 2004)

Pictures of the Dark (Gray Friar Press, 2009)

Let's Drink to the Dead (Solaris, 2012)

The Condemned (Gray Friar Press, 2013)

Chapbooks

Angels of the Silences (Pendragon Press, 2011)

Thin Men With Yellow Faces (with Gary McMahon) (This Is Horror, 2012)

Visit Simon Bestwick at his website:
simon-bestwick.blogspot.com